DEVIL'S BANE

DEVIL'S BANE

TALES OF A FOURTH GRADE WARRIOR

KEN MACGREGOR

Dragon's Roost Press

Devil's Bane: Tales of a Fourth Grade Warrior is published by Dragon's Roost Press.

Copyright © 2020 by Ken MacGregor

Cover art by Aurora Christie

All rights reserved.

All characters in this book are fictitious. Any resemblance to any persons living, dead, or otherwise animated is strictly coincidental.

Printed in the United States of America

First Printing, 2020

Paperback ISBN: 978-1-7351233-0-1

Dragon's Roost Press

207 Gardendale

Ferndale, MI 48220

For Elise MacGregor, who inspired the book.

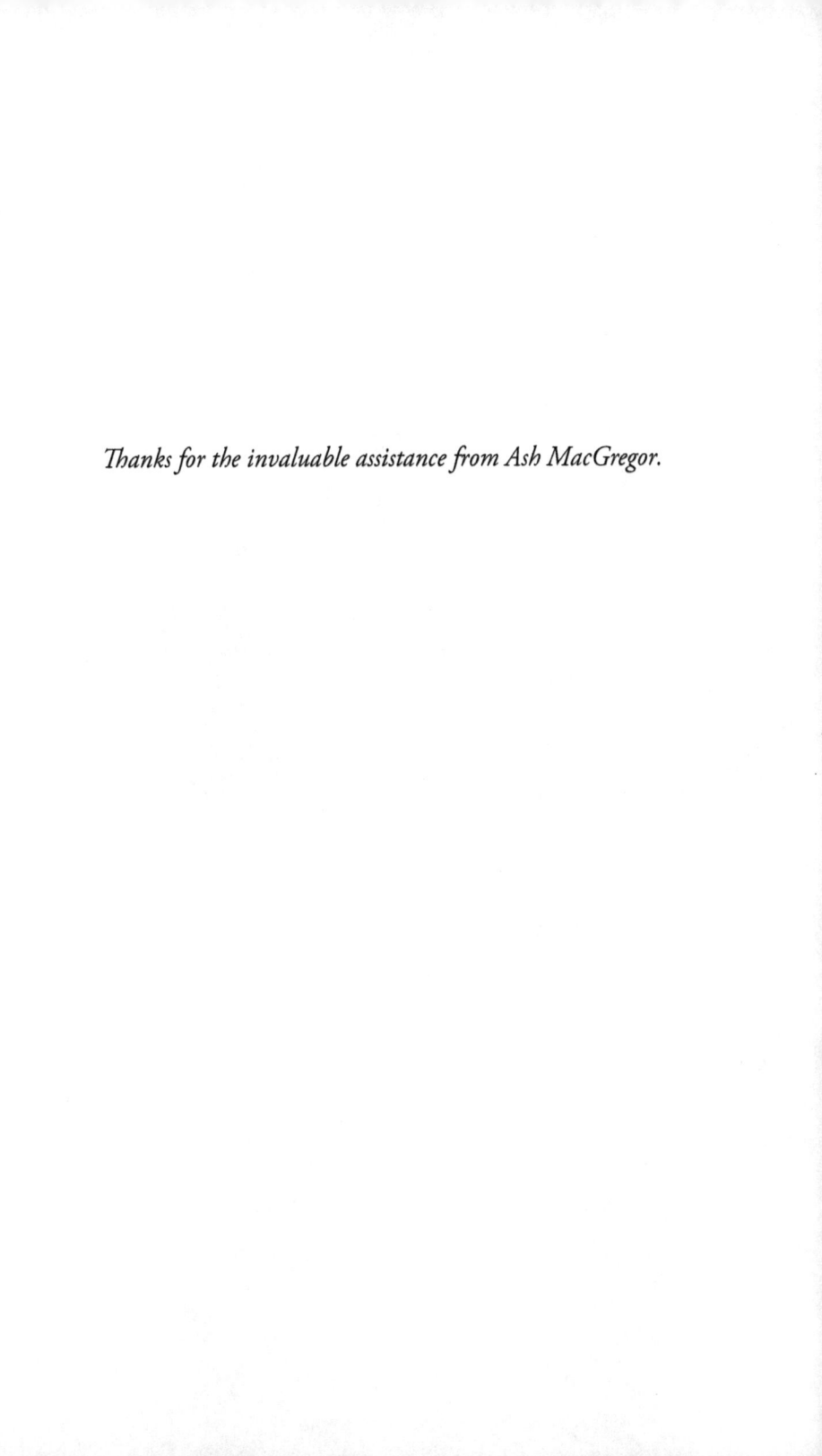

Thanks for the invaluable assistance from Ash MacGregor.

1

JOSH JUMPED OFF THE COUCH; it scrunched the rug and banged against the wall.

"Josh!" His mother, from the study.

"Sorry." He hit the floor running and burst outside.

His father got out of the car. His face, neck and clothes were splashed with blood.

Josh stopped, staring with wide eyes.

His dad smiled.

"Don't worry, kiddo. It's not mine."

"Oh good. What was it?"

"Hellhounds. Two of 'em."

"Wow! Can I come next time?"

His dad laughed. "One of these days, bud."

"Man," Josh said. "I never get to go on hunts."

His dad clapped him on the back. "Your turn will come, believe me. For now, though, I'd like to grab a shower and some dinner. I'm famished."

"Okay, Dad."

"Why's the couch over there?"

Josh grinned. "No idea."

2

JOSH AND CALEB pedaled like mad, wind in their faces, elm trees zipping by on either side.

Caleb was a half-foot ahead when they swooped into his driveway

"The winner!"

Josh put his feet down, grinning.

"Yep. You got me."

Caleb smiled and leaned forward, to catch his breath. Then, he picked up his bike.

As Caleb reached for the doorknob, it turned.

He yanked his hand back with a yelp.

Caleb's father stepped out, wearing only cut-offs and sneakers with no socks.

"Hey, fellas. I'm mowin' the lawn. It's a dirty job, but…"

"Someone has to do it," Caleb finished.

"There's a couple of root beers in the fridge still, if you want 'em."

Josh grinned. "Thank you, sir."

The man's eyebrows arched.

"'Sir'? I like this kid."

In the kitchen, Caleb handed Josh a bottle of Virgil's. It was, hands down, the best kind of root beer, both boys agreed. They popped the caps with twin hisses.

Outside, the lawnmower rattled and roared to life.

"Your dad's nice."

Caleb shrugged. "He's okay."

They drank deeply.

Josh looked out the window, then back at his friend.

"Where are his scars?"

The bottle in Caleb's hand froze on its way to his mouth.

"What do you mean?"

"His scars. You know. Dads have scars. Yours doesn't. It's weird."

Caleb slugged soda. He shook his head. "Josh, man, I don't think most dads have scars. It's not, like, a *thing*, you know? Your dad has some?"

Josh burped loudly. He grinned, and they both laughed. Josh patted his gut.

"Yeah. He's got a ton. Bites, bullet wounds, cuts, claw marks, burns. Um, other stuff. I forget the rest."

Caleb stared at him. "Your dad's been *shot*? And *stabbed*? And *bitten*?"

Josh nodded. "Yeah. Though, I think he's only ever been bitten twice. Pretty sure that's what he said."

"By what?"

Josh pouted a little. "He won't tell me. Says I'm too young." Caleb rinsed out the empty bottles and put them under the sink in the six-pack holder. There were close to fifty empties under there already. His family saved them up until they had enough to get ice cream. The ten-cent Michigan bottle deposit was always used for treats.

"I knew your dad was cool, but I've always wondered: what does he *do*?"

Josh looked at the floor. "I'm not supposed to talk about it."

"Dude, is he a spy?"

Josh scoffed. "No."

"Is he a soldier?"

"Yeah. Kinda. Maybe 'warrior' would be a better word."

"Cool."

Outside, Caleb's dad pushed the mower past the window. His shoulders and back already turning pink from the sun. He waved at the boys, who waved back.

"My dad seems pretty boring all of a sudden."

"Sometimes boring is better."

Caleb gave him a long look. "Is everything okay?"

Josh looked up. His eyes shone with unshed tears.

"I don't know."

3
———

Josh left the suburbs and cut loose, holding nothing back. By the end of the three miles to the small farm his family owned, he was doing forty.

He leaped off the bike, which kept going, slamming into the hedge. Against the odds, it stayed upright.

Josh was airborne, and his momentum carried him seven feet. He hit the ground, did a smooth shoulder-roll, and came up running.

He whooped as he skidded to a stop on the porch.

The door opened. His mom glanced at him, then at the bike in the bushes. Her mascara ran in thin, black lines to her chin, but her voice was steady.

"You better come in."

Josh's joy evaporated.

His dad slumped in the puffy green recliner, his head back, and eyes on the ceiling. His fingers dangled over the scratches in the fabric; they were all that was left of Bandit, whom Josh had called "Mr. Scrappy Cat." He had been hit by a car two years before.

Josh stood before the chair. His mom hovered in the doorway.

"Dad?"

His dad let out a long, tired sigh from his nose. "Yeah. Hi, kiddo."

Josh swallowed. "Dad, are you—is it…"

"It's bad, Josh."

The boy's face grew tight. He balled his hands into fists. Tears seeped from his eyes; he didn't sob. When he had himself mostly under control, he looked back up at his dad, who was watching him.

"Do you know how— " He choked, started again. "How long? Until…"

His dad shook his head. "

The doctor says maybe a year. "Eighteen months, tops."

Josh's chest hitched. Clear snot flowed from one nostril; he swiped it away with his wrist.

"That's not enough time, Dad. I'm not *ready*."

"We'll get you ready."

"I don't even mean *that*. I'm not ready to lose you."

His dad sighed. He gave his son a sad smile. "It's mutual, kid."

His mom put her arms around him, kneeling to hug him from behind. He hadn't heard her move, and he jumped. Josh could normally hear a spider crawling on the wall.

"Honey," she said, "your dad needs you to get serious about training now."

"This is stupid. Training is stupid. Dad being sick is stupid. *You're* stupid!"

He broke away from her and ran upstairs.

Josh sat, legs crossed under him, on his bed. He faced the window, looking at nothing.

Behind him, someone tapped shave-and-a-haircut on the doorframe. It was his dad.

Josh met his eyes, then looked away. "Sorry."

"It's okay, bud. People say things they don't mean when they're scared, or hurt, or angry."

Josh sniffed. "I think I'm all three." His dad eased himself onto Josh's bed. Josh leaned against him, and his dad kissed his head.

"I think I am too, bud."

Josh stared at him. "You get scared?"

His dad put his arm around his shoulder and squeezed him in a half hug. "Everybody gets scared. It's perfectly natural."

"But you hunt monsters, Dad. You're a genuine hero, like out of a comic book or something."

His dad chuckled. "Well, I don't know about all that, but I'll tell you one thing: when something's trying to kill me, I'm pretty much on the verge of peeing my pants. It's terrifying."

Josh processed this for a minute. "Then, why do it?"

"Because, Josh, I *can*. Someone has to, and I have the skills, training and talent for it. My father had the same gifts, and he taught me."

Josh drew a tissue from the box. He blew his nose loudly, and they both smiled at the cartoon sound of it.

"And, you're going to teach me, right?"

His dad half-hugged him again. "That's the idea."

Josh sighed, twice. The second one was big, drawn out. "I really want to try out for soccer this year, Dad."

"I know."

"I think I could be good. Maybe great."

His dad rubbed Josh's back in small circles with his fingertips. It was how he'd calmed his son since he was tiny. "What position?"

Josh looked up at him, hopeful. "Forward."

"Wow. Lots of running."

"I know. I like running. I'm fast."

"Yeah. I know. I've seen you run."

They were quiet for a time. Josh enjoyed the feel of his dad's fingers on his back.

"Dad?"

"Hm?"

"Do you think I could train with you, *and* go out for soccer? You know, do both?"

His dad looked thoughtful. His hand stopped. "Well…you'd have to keep up with your schoolwork."

"I would."

"And the chores around the farm."

"I know."

"And, training comes first. Before soccer, I mean. If there's a game, but I need you to run a special mission, you *skip* the game. Understood?"

Josh nodded. "Yes, sir."

His dad smiled. "I'll try not to put you in that position if I can help it."

Josh smiled. "Thanks, Dad."

"There's a catch, bud."

Josh swallowed hard. "What?"

"Between school, soccer, and training with me, the only things you're going to have time for are eating and sleeping. This means no time with friends, no time to play. This is not something I would ask you to give up."

"But you kind of are. Asking, I mean."

His dad smiled at him. "True. I don't want to, though. Josh, I wouldn't wish this kind of life on anyone. I sure as hell didn't want it when I was a kid."

Josh's eyes widened, both at the curse word, and the thought that his dad was once a little kid facing the same thing he was now.

"Dad?"

"Yeah?"

"What did you have to give up?"

His father stared through the wall, maybe at some distant memory. His voice, when he answered, was a hoarse whisper.

"Everything."

Josh stared at his father's profile for a long time. "Dad?"

"Mm?"

"Mom's not stupid. I shouldn't have said that."

"I know. Whattya say we go tell her you didn't mean it?"

"Yeah. Okay."

4

JOSH'S THOUGHTS kept cycling back to the same place: *a year-and-a-half, maybe less.* Numb, he moved from his classroom to the art room down the hall. Usually, he hurried to art; it was his third favorite part of the day, after recess and gym. They were currently making clay pots by hand.

But, today, he shuffled along the orange and yellow tiles, not wanting to go to art, or anywhere else, not wanting to do anything.

As he was passing Simon Woods, a fifth grader, the much larger boy's foot shot out, tripping Josh.

He caught himself on his palms, but his notebook slid across the shiny linoleum.

Josh blinked up at Simon. "Why did you do that?"

Simon loomed close. "Why don't you watch where you're going, *little* kid?"

"I don't—" Josh's eyes widened. "Oh. I get it. You're being mean to me because you're bigger."

Simon paused and stared at him for a few seconds. Clearly, this was not going as he expected. "Why don't you pick up your little pansy notebook and run crying to your teacher?"

Josh retrieved his notebook, stood up, and tilted his head to look at the bigger boy.

"It's Simon, right?" Simon blinked and nodded. "Okay. I get that you wanna be a tough guy. You want respect. Scaring people is easy. Respect takes work. That's what my dad says, and he's one to know, believe me."

Simon's eyebrows bunched up. His scowl bent almost to his chin. He leaned even closer. Their noses were almost touching. Simon stabbed him in the chest with a finger and spoke in a harsh whisper.

"After school, I'll be waiting for you. And, none of your talk is gonna stop me from beating the snot out of you. I'll make you swallow your words, and some of your teeth, too."

He whirled away and strutted down the hall.

Josh called after him. "Looking forward to it!"

Mr. Bagley, the fourth-grade teacher, strolled by and shushed him.

Josh spent the entire art class shaping monsters out of clay and whispering their names to himself.

When Mr. Roth saw him, he chuckled. "Everybody has their own process, Josh. I can see you're trying something new here. Good for you."

THE REST of the school day trudged by until the final bell. Josh shoved everything into his desk, except the notebook and the book on Greek Mythology he had to study for homework. These, he slid into his backpack, flipping the strap over one shoulder.

On the front lawn, a circle of third, fourth, and fifth graders surrounded Simon. A low murmur spread through the crowd as they spotted Josh.

He set down his bag, striding into the ring of kids. It closed behind him. He caught Simon's eye. "Last chance to walk away."

Simon snorted. "I don't think so."

"Okay," said Josh. "Don't say I didn't warn you."

"Shut up."

Josh nodded. "Okay."

Simon stepped in, swinging his fist from way back. He was big for eleven, and if it had connected, it likely would have hurt.

Josh was somehow an inch out of range. Simon stumbled, but kept his feet.

He swung again. And again.

Simon was out of breath after a short time. He panted, hands on bent knees.

Josh smiled at him. "Are you done?"

"No. If you. Just. Hold still."

He swung and missed again.

"Okay. Tell you what. I'll hold still and let you hit me. But then I get to hit you back. Deal?"

"Uh huh."

Simon lunged as soon as he spoke. He clocked Josh across the cheekbone.

The smaller boy fell on his tailbone. The punch hurt a lot more than he expected. His cheek was hot with pain and embarrassment.

Simon shook out his hand, clearly feeling the hit, too.

Josh shook it off, got to his feet, and studied Simon. He raised an open palm high above his head.

Simon glanced at it.

Josh slammed his foot into Simon's gut, knocking the wind out of him.

Simon writhed on the ground, gasping for air.

Josh squatted next to him and spoke quietly. "I'm sorry."

The circle broke to let him out. A strange kid handed him his backpack.

"Do you know Karate?"

Josh considered his response. The truth was complicated, and dangerous. "Yeah. Something like that."

The boy, another big fifth grader, put up surrender-palms

and smiled. "That's cool. I don't think Simon's going to give you any more trouble. I don't think *anyone* will."

Josh shook his head. "I didn't want to hurt him. I'm not supposed to hurt people."

5

CALEB WOULDN'T FACE HIM. Josh could tell his friend was crying, but he wasn't about to give him a hard time. Caleb sniffed. "You gotta tell me *why* at least."

"I can't."

"Why not?"

Josh sighed. "It's my dad. He's really sick." Josh could feel his own tears coming, but he went on. "He's dying, man."

"Oh my god."

Josh nodded. They sat, silently crying, two nine-year-old boys fumbling to grasp mortality.

Caleb wiped his nose. He swiped the tears from his face and turned to Josh. "But, why can't we be friends? I'm real sorry about your dad, man, but I biked all the way out here, and you owe me some kind of explanation."

Josh gave him a long, considering look. "Can I trust you? To keep a secret, I mean."

"Of course."

"You can't tell *anybody*, Caleb. I'm not playing around."

Caleb nodded. "I promise."

Josh held up his right hand, crooked pinkie extended. "Pinkie-swear."

Caleb solemnly hooked his pinkie around Josh's. "I pinkie-swear it."

Josh told him the truth. He talked about monster hunters and the balance between good and evil, and how his dad was a part of it all, and how Josh was training to take his place.

"So, your dad really *is* a warrior."

"Yeah. And, now I have to be one. To replace my dad when…when he's gone. And, training is *hard*, Caleb. It's going to take all my spare time."

Caleb thought about this for a while. "But you're still going out for soccer." Josh nodded. "So, you're telling me that playing soccer is more important than spending time with me."

Josh shook his head. "No, you big jerk. I'm telling you that saving the world is more important than anything else in my life."

"Except soccer." Caleb sulked.

"Caleb, stop busting my butt. You *know* how important soccer is to me."

"Yeah. I know. I also know what a good imagination you have. You're good at making stuff up. Always have been. Really good."

The words sounded complimentary, but Caleb's voice was dripping with sarcasm.

Josh stared at him. His jaw clenched. "You think I'm lying."

"I totally believe you about your dad dying. Nobody would pretend that. But, come on, man. The monster hunter stuff? Really, Josh?"

Josh lifted the collar of his T-shirt and wiped away the few tears on his cheeks. When he turned to his friend, his expression was fierce, defiant. "I can prove it."

"What?"

"I can prove that monsters are real. I'll summon one and fight it. I started training a few months ago. I can handle myself."

Caleb scoffed. "A monster? For real? Right here in your

bedroom, in your little farmhouse, you're going to summon an honest-to-goodness monster?"

"No. Not here." He stood. "In the bathroom."

JOSH LIT the candle and turned off the bathroom light. His hand hardly trembled at all. A chemical pine scent filled the small room.

Caleb touched Josh's wrist with his fingertips, so lightly it gave him goosebumps.

He whispered. "Do you really think it'll work?"

Josh shrugged. He was whispering, too. "It's supposed to."

Caleb smiled nervously. "I kind of hope it doesn't."

Josh nodded, looked at the big wall mirror and then back at him. "Yeah. We need to do this quick, before my dad wonders what we're up to."

"Why? Is he super strict?"

Josh snorted. It was loud in the enclosed space. The smoke from the candle was making his eyes water, so he set it down by the sink. "No. But, he says I shouldn't 'mess around with the supernatural.'" He did air quotes. "He says I'm too young. Whatever."

He was trying to sound cool, casual. He took a big breath and faced the mirror again. He put a hand on Caleb's shoulder. "You ready?"

He nodded.

Together, they chanted. "Bloody Mary. Bloody Mary. Bloody Mary."

For a moment, nothing happened. Josh sighed, and his shoulders drooped. *Figures.*

Then, from the center of the mirror, concentric circles rippled out, as if the glass was a liquid that someone had touched.

Caleb gasped.

Josh gulped. "Whoa."

The candle went out. Both kids screamed.

In the dark, they each grabbed handfuls of the other's shirt and clung to each other.

From the wall mirror, there was a *squelch*. Then dripping. The chemical pine scent was overwhelmed by a new smell, like sucked-on pennies. The dripping intensified until it was more of a splatter.

Hot fluid hit their bare arms and necks.

Both kids cried, quietly as they could, and waited to die.

Something tugged on Josh's hair. He pictured a harpy's talons protruding from filthy, stinking feathers. His scalp felt like it was going to tear.

The bathroom door slammed open and the room filled with blinding light. Josh's dad filled the doorway, hand on the switch.

Thank God, Josh thought.

The dead woman was halfway out of the mirror. Her hollow cheeks framed a lamprey mouth, round and sucking, filled with tiny, grasping teeth.

Seeing the adult, she whipped her head around to look at him. Her flat eyes went wide. She let go of Josh's hair with her clawed hand. A chunk of it caught on a claw and came out.

Josh whimpered and grabbed the spot.

The man held the monstrous woman's gaze. His lip twitched. He shook his head. "Damn it, Josh."

The big man lunged across the room. His left fist smashed into Bloody Mary's jaw, knocking out dozens of the sharp teeth. They clattered into the sink.

She howled and raised her arms defensively as the man rained blows on her ribs and gut. She swiped a clawed hand at him, but he slapped it aside and hit her with the other hand.

New, fresh blood splattered across the counter and stained the hand towels.

He'd broken her nose. Both her eyes were swelling shut. Her right cheekbone was concave. She was no longer a terrifying monster; she was a wounded animal.

With a reptile hiss, Mary pulled herself back through the mirror. It made a slurping *pop.*

She was gone.

Josh's father pulled a terrycloth towel off the rack and wiped the blood off his hands.

He turned to look at his son and Caleb, still huddled on the floor. "How many times do I have to tell you not to mess with stuff like this?"

"Sorry, Dad."

"Sorry's not good enough. No screen time for a month. Now, clean this up. There's a bottle of bleach under the sink."

He nodded to Caleb and walked out.

Caleb untangled himself from Josh and pushed himself up using the wall. Turning huge eyes to Josh, he stammered. "I can't. I don't. That's impossible." Josh nodded.

"I know, right? No screen time for *a month?* That's not fair."

He snatched the white bleach bottle and the big sponge and sighed. He gestured to his friend with them, looked at the blood covering everything, and gave him a 'help me?' kind of smile.

Caleb shook his head. He looked a bit green. "I should go."

He went.

Josh grumbled and wet the sponge.

"Guess I'll clean it up myself then."

He poured some bleach on the sponge and wiped at the bloody counter. He stopped when he noticed the teeth in the sink. Picking one up, he turned it in his fingers, careful not to touch the point. The dull end had three small prongs that must have held it in her gums. Some teeth had fallen into the drain but were hung up on the stainless-steel trap. He had to use tweezers to retrieve them. Finally, he collected a small pile of them on a few squares of T.P.

It took forever to clean up the mess. No way was he doing *that* again.

6

SOCCER TRYOUTS WERE CROWDED. It looked like half the fourth grade was trying to make the team.

Caleb was there, but he wasn't trying out. When he caught Josh's eye, he shot Josh a thumbs-up, but he didn't smile. He still looked a bit stunned from the bathroom thing.

Though there were players there with more experience, Josh did well. He ran faster than all but one boy, who was tall for nine, and most of it legs. Josh picked up dribbling quickly and made accurate passes more often than not.

He held himself back, of course. With his superior strength, speed, and reflexes, Josh could've played soccer with adults. But, as his dad liked to point out, blending in was a survival skill.

He made the team without raising any eyebrows. Which was good. The fight with Simon had made people talk about him. Pretty much everyone gave him a wide berth, even the bigger, tougher kids. Kids his own age clapped him on the back and said things like, "way to go." So, he didn't need anything else drawing attention to him.

So far, at least, the teachers seemed oblivious. Of course, grown-ups could be sneaky. When you think they're clueless, sometimes they've been onto you all along.

Josh parked his bike at the edge of the driveway and propped it on the kickstand. Ms. Bagley was across the street, watering her begonias. It wouldn't be prudent to leap off the bike doing twenty-five miles an hour.

He smiled and waved, and she returned it with a floral-gloved hand. Her side of the street used to be all farmland too, but she had sold most of it, and it had been broken up into lots. The frames of houses-to-be were popping up all over. His dad grumbled a lot about losing their privacy.

He held the doorknob for half-a-minute before turning it.

His parents were at the dining room table. His mom was drinking coffee and his dad was reading Bram Stoker's Dracula; he read it every year.

Both looked at him, expectant.

Josh milked the moment, keeping his face blank for as long as he could stand to. The grin broke free.

"I made the team!"

Smiles, hugs, congratulations, and ice cream followed, in that order.

It was a good day. It was the last really good day Josh had for a long, long time.

7

THERE WAS a forty-five-minute gap between his last class and soccer practice. Josh spent it reading a book of Ray Bradbury's short stories. The man had been good friends with another monster hunter, and many of his stories were based in fact. He was required reading for all monster hunters in training, but Josh loved the stories and would have read them regardless.

A shadow fell across the book. He looked up. An adult he didn't recognize stood before him, smiling. The woman was classically beautiful, with dark skin, sharp cheekbones, curled black hair, cut short, and eyes so dark they might as well have been all pupil.

"Good book?"

Josh nodded. He slid the bookmark into place and closed it without taking his eyes off the stranger. "Something I can help you with...ma'am?"

Her smile widened. Josh noted the pronounced canines.

"You know? I believe there is. I'm an old friend of your father's, Josh. We go way back. Since he was younger than you, in fact."

He narrowed his eyes. "You don't look much older than my art teacher, who's, um, twenty-four, I think."

"I'm told I look good for my age."

Josh set down the book and stood up. She was taller, but he was a little closer to eye-to-eye now.

"Well," he said, "you're out here in broad daylight, so you can't be a vampire. What are you?"

She gave him wide, shocked eyes, and fanned herself with one hand. But, the corner of her lips curved up, and her eyes danced with amusement. "So forward. So blunt. Truly, you are your father's son."

"I have soccer practice in about twenty minutes. You have fifteen to tell me what you want from me."

"I am impressed, Josh. You come across as very grown-up and authoritative. All right, I'll be straight with you. My name, though it will likely mean nothing to you, is Leandra. Your family and I go a long ways back. I knew your father's father, and that man's father, and his, too. Generations of Campbells. All strong, determined, powerful men. All courageous fighters for Good. Each and every one of them a thorn in my proverbial side."

Josh cocked an eyebrow. It was a skill he had picked up that year.

"You're evil."

"Only *technically*, Josh."

"I know how this works. You're here to try to sway me to the darkness, right? Not gonna happen."

Her smile sparkled. "Oh, no. I know better. I can see, just by looking at you, that you are pure of heart, just like your father."

"Then why are you here? What do you want?"

"I'm here to make you an offer. Your father's cancer is inoperable. The doctors can't save his life." She paused. "I can."

Josh stared into the blackness of her eyes. He believed her. For a long time, he considered his words. "What's the price?"

She smiled broadly. She was quite pretty when smiling, like shattered glass sparkling in the sun. "Nothing."

"Wait. What?"

"That's my price. Nothing. You do nothing. No training. No hunting. No combating the darkness. You live your life as a normal boy: ride your bike, play soccer, hang out with friends. *Kid* stuff. And, nothing else."

Across the field, the coach hauled a huge, net bag full of soccer balls out from the shed.

Josh thought about what life might be like as a monster hunter. Always in danger, always a target. How he'd be afraid to make friends or have a family (unless he married someone super-tough, like his father had. He wasn't entirely sure his mom was even human). He thought about being a normal kid, with no pressure to be anything else, anything *more*. "How long do I have? To think about it, I mean? To decide?"

She touched his chin with the tips of her fingers. They were hot, like she was running a dangerous fever. "My dear boy, you have a year. A year and a half, tops."

8

JOSH KEPT his gloves up to protect his face. He bobbed and weaved. He kept his eyes on his dad. He did everything he was supposed to.

Still, his father landed blow after blow.

Josh stepped back, hands high. It was their signal to stop the fight.

His dad, who was not even winded, sighed. "What?"

"I'm not learning how to fight. I'm your punching bag."

"Son, part of learning to fight is learning how to take a hit. Besides, you *are* learning. Two months ago, you couldn't remember to keep your hands up. You stood still and let me pummel you."

Josh sulked. "You're still pummeling me."

His dad tilted his head. He untied the laces of his right glove with his teeth. When he had both gloves off, he untied his son's. "What's really bothering you, Josh?"

"Nothing."

"Come on, kid. I've known you your whole life. I can tell when something's weighing on your mind. What's up?"

Josh wiped sweat from his upper lip. He looked at the floor

mats. They were woven tightly, from Japan. *Tatami*, he remembered. *That's what they're called.*

Realizing he was looking for distractions, he forced himself to meet his father's eyes. "I'm not sure I'm allowed to tell you."

His dad's brows shot up. "Huh," was all he said.

Neither spoke for several seconds. Josh shuffled his feet on the tatami. It sounded like autumn leaves rustling.

"Have you ever heard of someone called Leandra?"

His dad's face was stone. "Where did you hear that name?"

"Um, from her?"

His dad's eyes narrowed to slits. "You met Leandra, in the flesh?"

Josh considered this. "I'm pretty sure she was really there, yeah. She touched my face. Her fingers were super-hot, like she was burning up with fever. She also smelled kind of like cloves."

His dad shot him a wide-eyed glance. "Cloves."

Josh nodded. Then, his dad used a word Josh had never heard him use before. It was a word the middle-school kids used sometimes, but never when the teachers were around. It was said under his breath, but Josh caught it.

"Dad! That's a bad word."

His dad shot him a rueful smile. "No, kiddo. It's just a word. It's not one you should use at school, or around your grandparents, but it's not a *bad* word. There are words of power; words that can cause pain; words that can kill. *Those* are bad words."

Josh thought about this for a while. He smiled at his dad. "So … I can swear if I want?"

His dad shook his head and smiled back. "You're too smart for my own good, kid. Sure, you can swear. But, not around your mother, okay?"

Josh put out his hand, and his dad shook it.

"Deal." He picked up his gloves. "You wanna beat me up some more?"

His dad put up a restraining palm. "Tell me about Leandra. What did she offer you?"

Josh's jaw fell open. "How did you—"

"It's what she does. She makes deals. And, they are always, *always* to her advantage. Now, what did she say to you?"

Josh looked at his feet. "She said she could cure you."

His dad chewed on the inside of his lip. "Right. That makes sense. What would you have to do? For my cure, I mean. What did she want in return?"

Josh looked up at his dad. He couldn't believe they were discussing his father's potential death so casually. Tears filled his eyes. "I'd have to give up training. Not hunt monsters. Just be a normal kid."

His dad nodded. He was looking through the basement wall, to a place or memory maybe, somewhere far from here. "And?"

Josh sniffed. "And what?"

"Can you do that?"

"I don't know, Dad."

Josh was crying now. Sobs pushed their way out, despite him trying hard to hold them back.

His dad knelt and hugged him.

Josh dropped the sparring gloves and put his arms around his father's neck. He inhaled the scent of the man's sweat, and his fingers traced the familiar pattern of scars on his shoulders and upper back.

"I love you, Josh. No matter what happens. I want you to know that."

Josh spoke into his shoulder. "I love you, too."

His dad stroked his hair with a calloused hand. His skin felt as tough as leather.

"Josh?"

"Mm?"

"Did she say how long you have to decide?"

"Yeah. I asked that, too. She basically said I had as long as you're still around."

His dad nodded. "Okay. This is good. Gives us some time. I can focus on your training. Teach you how to deal, or rather, how *not* to deal with demons. That's usually late-stage stuff, but the order doesn't matter, not really."

Josh stepped back on the mat. He looked at his dad, wide-eyed. His dad's hand still hung in the air, fingers parted, mid-hair stroke. He let it drop and arched an eyebrow, waiting.

"Leandra is a *demon*? An actual demon from Hell came to my school and offered to save your life?"

His dad put up both palms and shook his head. "Whoa. Hold on a minute. Nobody said anything about 'Hell.' Let's not get all crazy with the Christianity stuff."

Josh pressed his lips together. "Well, where else do demons come from?"

His dad let his head drop for a moment. When he looked up, he gave his son a tight smile. "Okay. Lesson one about demons: the word 'demon' is a convenient, if over-used, term for any extra-dimensional being with malevolent intent."

"I didn't understand at least half of what you just said."

"Sorry," his dad said, smiling. "Demons are basically nasty creatures, from somewhere other than Earth (as we know it), who have varying degrees of power. Some of them can only play minor pranks, like hiding your keys. Some, well, some demons could turn whole cities to ash."

Josh thought about this. "Where does Leandra fall in the power-level thing?"

"Closer to the city/ash end of the spectrum, though not quite there."

"If she's so tough, why didn't she just kill me? Problem solved."

His dad shook his head. "Self-preservation, mostly. If she kills you, a child, every single monster hunter in the world would come after her. If we worked together, she wouldn't stand a chance."

"So, she can't kill me. I don't have to worry about her."

"You *do* have to worry. She's dangerous, Josh, and not to be trusted."

Josh rolled his eyes. "Well, duh."

9

AFTER HIS SHOWER, Josh ran downstairs in his underwear.

"Mom! Dad! Check it out." He looked down at himself as he tensed his muscles. "Two, four, six, eight. I have an eight-pack!"

His dad chuckled. "Those bottom two don't really count. Nice six-pack though."

Josh looked crestfallen, but he rallied. "A six-pack is still pretty sweet," he said. "Just like you, Dad. Whattya think, Mom?"

"You're beautiful, and very fit. Now, go put on some pants."

Once he was all the way dressed, Josh put away three scrambled eggs, toast, two glasses of orange juice, and a corn muffin.

His mother elbowed his dad. "He eats like you now."

His dad grinned. "Just wait 'til he's a teenager; you'll be grocery shopping every day."

Josh and his mother stared at him. The humor fell from his face as what he said sank in. *You'll* have to. Because he wouldn't be around.

He took a deep, shuddering breath and let it out. "Come on, Josh. I'll drop you at school. I need to run some errands downtown."

His mom gave his dad a look Josh couldn't read. He was pretty sure it wasn't a good look, though. As his dad kissed her on the corner of her mouth, Josh wondered what the mysterious errands might be, and why they upset his mom.

Somehow, he was certain that asking either of them about it was a bad idea. Pretending not to notice any of this, he brushed his teeth, slipped into his perpetually tied sneakers, and threw his backpack on one shoulder.

"Ready."

They drove to the school in silence, both lost in their own thoughts. Josh leaned in the window after getting out, and hugged his dad around the neck.

"Good luck."

His dad raised an eyebrow. "With what?"

Josh shrugged. "With whatever you're doing today. I don't know what it is, but I can tell it's important. So, good luck."

His dad smiled and shook his head. "Sometimes, kid, I forget how sharp you are. That may save your life someday. Probably more than a few times. Thank you. I'll take all the luck I can get. Have a good day at school, bud. See you this afternoon. I'm gonna show you those joint locks I was telling you about."

Josh grinned. "Cool."

He jogged up the steps, backpack thumping. At the doors, he turned, just in time to see his dad's brake lights disappearing around the corner.

10

Conversations in the cafeteria blurred into one loud background sound.

Josh wolfed down his tuna salad sandwich. He ate the carrot and celery at a more sedate pace.

He felt someone's attention and looked up.

Simon stood at a respectful distance, tray in his hand. The school's hot lunch, pizza with cardboard crust, steamed on it.

"Hey," Simon said.

"Hey."

"Is it okay if I sit here?

Josh shrugged. "Sure."

For a long time, they ate without speaking. In his peripheral vision, Josh saw Simon sneaking glances at him. He sighed, stuffed his empty containers in the thermal bag, and the bag in his backpack. He met the larger boy's gaze.

"What's going on, Simon?"

"Not much."

"It looks like you're dying to say something to me. Why don't you say it?"

Simon finished chewing. He swallowed. He wiped his

mouth with a paper napkin that was already peppered with pizza sauce.

"I talked to Caleb."

Josh tried to keep the surprise and worry from his face, with little success. "Okay."

Simon swallowed. He looked around and leaned in conspiratorially. "He told me about Bloody Mary."

Josh clenched his teeth. His hands balled into fists. He forced himself to breathe through it and relax. It took a while.

"You believed him?"

Simon nodded. "He was pretty shook up by the whole thing, and he told me details, too. Stuff so weird, I just can't believe he made it up."

"The teeth?"

Simon grimaced. "Yeah. That's what convinced me. What did you do with them anyway?"

"I kept 'em. Got a little wooden box on my dresser. It's got a hinged lid. It's about—" He held his hands half-a-foot apart. "—this big. I keep stuff in there. Special stuff, you know?"

"Yeah. I got one, too. Mine's a cigar box, though. Smells like cedar. Mostly, I keep Magic cards in it. I don't play anymore, but I used to be crazy into the game."

Josh considered this. "I guess probably everybody has something like that, huh?"

"Yeah. I guess. Never really thought about it before."

"Me either."

They were quiet. Josh picked a piece of celery out of his teeth with a fingernail. Simon finished his lunch.

"So, you're telling me about Caleb because…"

"Your dad fights monsters. Caleb said you were training to do it, too."

"Caleb has a big mouth." Simon shrugged. "Yeah. I am."

Simon nodded. "I want in."

"What?"

"I want to be a monster hunter. I want to protect people from bad guys. I wanna be a hero, Josh."

"Simon, it's not that simple."

"Why not?"

Josh's shoulders slumped. "My dad and I, we were *born* to do this. We're stronger, faster, and tougher than most people. It's why I was able to beat you so easily, even though you're bigger than me."

"That actually kind of makes me feel better."

"Yeah. I bet."

"But I still want to do it. I messed up, picking on you. Not because you beat me, though that's what it took to make me realize. But, because it was the wrong thing to do, the wrong way to be. I want to be tough, sure, but I want to be one of the good guys, you know? Like Spider-Man or something. I don't care if I'm just a regular kid. I can still train. I can learn how to fight. Get tough enough to hold my own. Like Bruce Lee."

"Bruce Lee."

"Yeah. He was only human and look what he did." Simon paused. "Wait. He was human, right?"

Josh shrugged. "As far as I know."

Simon grinned. "Well, there you go. If he could do it, so can I."

Josh gave him a small smile. "You know? That's a pretty good argument. Only problem is, Simon, that I don't think my dad is gonna be willing to train you."

Simon rubbed his earlobe between his thumb and forefinger. After a while, his face lit up. "*You* can train me. Whatever your dad teaches you, you pass on to me. Problem solved."

For a long moment, Josh looked at him. The constant hum of other kids' conversations, of paper bags crinkling, faded into a dull, hazy throb. It was as if Josh were on a plane, and the cabin pressure dropped, plugging up his ears. His own voice, when he spoke, sounded muffled and distant.

"I'm sorry, Simon. I get what you're trying to do. I think it's great that you want to be a hero. But I just don't have time."

Simon's head dropped. His chin rested on his chest. But, when he came back up, he was smiling.

"It's okay. I get it. I knew it was probably a long shot, but I had to ask. It's not going to discourage me, you know. I've made up my mind about this. I'll just have to find someone else to train me."

Josh returned his smile. He put out his hand. Simon took it, and they shook.

"I hope you do," he said. "The world needs more heroes."

"Heroes like you."

Josh shook his head. "I'm not a hero, Simon. I'm just a kid who's had some crazy stuff dropped in his lap. It's not like I have a choice. I was born into this."

Simon rested his hand on Josh's shoulder.

"Everybody always has choices, man. That's what my old man is always saying. I mean, if someone offered you a way out, would you take it?"

"Someone already has."

"Whoa. You said 'no,' right?"

Josh shook his head. "I didn't answer."

"Why not?"

"My dad's dying. She said she can save him, but I'd have to give up fighting monsters. It's a crazy choice to have to make."

"Oh man. Sorry about your dad. How long does he have?"

"A year. Maybe more. Not two."

Simon shook his head. "And, here I thought *my* life was a crap-and-cheese sandwich."

Josh managed a weak smile. "'Crap-and-cheese' — I like that."

Simon grinned. "Thanks." He got serious. "Listen, if that person, whoever she is, wants you to quit, you probably shouldn't. I mean, I get that losing your dad would be horrible. My big brother was killed by a drunk driver two years ago.

Death sucks. But, listen, Josh: if she's evil, and I think we both know she is, then you can't do the thing she wants."

"I know. I get that. But this is my *dad*. I don't know how I could live without him."

Simon nodded. "Yeah. But you get past it, man. I never would've believed I could talk about Nick without losing it, but I can. For almost a year now, I've been able to. It still hurts, and I still miss him every single day, but life goes on, you know?"

"I'm sorry about your brother."

"Thanks for that. I'm sorry about your dad. You know: in advance."

Josh shook his head. "The thing I don't get is—why did Leandra come to me?"

"I don't know. Leandra's the bad guy, right?" Josh nodded. "Maybe she came to you because she saw something in you. Something dangerous to her, or to her kind. You know: monsters. Maybe you're the Chosen One."

Josh laughed.

"Come on, Simon. This isn't Avatar; I'm not the Last Airbender. I'm just a kid."

"Last Airbender was just a kid, too." He grinned. "That's all I'm sayin'.

11

BEHIND THEIR MODEST, two-bedroom farmhouse, Josh's family owned six acres of land. The front yard was lawn. Right out back, a rusting swing set creaked in the breeze. Beyond that, corn and soy on rotation, and a large, fenced-in vegetable garden. A dirt road led to an enormous barn. Hidden inside was an almost military-grade obstacle course.

Josh had played here, of course. He'd found it when he was five, when he had gone in there looking for horses.

He had brought Caleb there, too, but swore him to secrecy. They used to play Pirates, Zombie Apocalypse, and a bunch of other games. It was where they played every time it rained.

One time, when they pushed open the big sliding wooden door, Josh's dad was moving across the course at inhuman speed.

He flipped, rolled, jumped, and spun with more grace than a gold-medal gymnast. Landing on the balls of his feet, he sprang up and beat the crap out of a practice dummy. His fists sounded like a sledgehammer hitting sandbags.

They gaped at him. He stopped.

As they watched, the man got his breath under control. Still facing away from them, he spoke.

"Hi, boys."

"Hey, Dad."

Caleb stared at Josh. He returned his gaze to Josh's dad. "How—how did you know we were here?"

He turned and smiled at Caleb. "Heard you coming outside. Your feet crunching in the leaves; your breathing; the whisper of denim sleeves as you swung your arms; your heartbeats."

Caleb gulped.

Josh tapped him with the back of his hand. "Don't believe him. He can't hear heartbeats. Dad's just showing off."

His dad shrugged.

"How do you know?" Caleb asked.

"Because *I* can't hear heartbeats. Unless it's very, very quiet where we are. Like, totally silent."

Caleb looked at the man in sweatpants and a T-shirt. It was a crisp October day; the temperature in the barn hovered around 50, but he seemed comfortable.

"Mr. Campbell? Are you a superhero?"

The man laughed.

"No, Caleb. I'm not a superhero. I'm a fighter, I guess. I use this area to train, to stay in shape, to stay sharp. Because, I never know when I might need it."

Caleb looked around at the equipment. He looked at his best friend, whose dad could do amazing things. "You don't have to worry about me telling anyone, Mr. Campbell. For one thing, I already pinkie-swore I'd keep this place a secret. For another, I mean, who would believe me?"

"Very few would," said Josh's dad. "And, those who would believe you are the kinds of folks you should probably avoid. All right, boys. I'm going to go grab a shower. This place is all yours."

After watching his dad be amazing on the obstacle course, Josh didn't feel like playing there. They sat on the bottom rung of a horizontal rope ladder.

"I have a few dollars," Caleb said. "We could bike over to Murphy's and get a couple of comic books."

Murphy's was an old-fashioned five-and-dime, a Woolworth's in all but name. It was in town, four miles from Josh's house.

Josh shook his head. "I already got this month's *Teen Titans*. That's the only title I'm reading these days."

"Can I look at it?"

"Sure. Come on in. I'll ask my mom if she can make us some mac 'n' cheese."

12

———

"Josh."

His eyes snapped open. A second later, he came fully awake. The digital clock read 3:17. His dad, already dressed, leaned over the bed.

"Dad? What's going on?"

"Black Hodag. Sighted in the woods, twelve miles from here. We're the closest. Get dressed."

Josh threw his pajamas in the hamper, pulled on underwear and jeans, and stopped.

"Wait. Doesn't the Hodag live in Wisconsin? What's it doing here?"

"Good memory. My contact thinks someone was transporting it, probably to sell it. There's a thriving black market for rare beasts."

Josh struggled into his shirt. It was not cooperating. "Makes sense."

He got his socks on and followed his dad to the front door. As he stepped into his shoes, the elder Campbell filled him in on the rest.

"Now, the Green Hodag, by far the most common breed, isn't dangerous. At worst, their mischief leads to misunderstandings and the occasional fistfight. But, the Black Hodag is bigger, meaner, and hard to control. Whoever caught it was taking a terrible risk. Since it got free, we can probably assume they are already dead, or will be soon."

Josh froze with his second shoe half on.

"Dead?"

His father hunkered and put his hands on Josh's shoulders.

"Not everyone is cut out for handling monsters, Josh. People, *ordinary* people, can get hurt, even killed."

Josh forced his heel into his sneaker. "Not us, though, right? Because we're tough?"

"We are tough, kiddo. But, we have to be *smart*, too. Running blindly into battle won't end well; I don't care who you are."

They climbed into his dad's Subaru; it had all-wheel drive and could fit where a lot of trucks wouldn't.

"Buckle up."

Josh did. So did his dad.

They drove north, through town and onto the highway.

"Okay," Josh said. "How do we fight a Black Hodag?"

His dad glanced at him, before putting his eyes back on the road. "Is that the right question?"

Josh mulled this over. "Okay…How about this: what are we going to *do* with the Hodag, once we get there?"

"Good. Any thoughts on that?"

Josh took a big breath. It occurred to him that he was alert, not tired at all, even though he had been yanked from a deep sleep.

"As I see it, we either have to catch it or kill it. It's an animal, right? So, we can't exactly talk to it."

His dad nodded. "That's true."

Josh watched the trees shoot by in the dark.

"*Can* we catch it safely, without getting hurt too much?"

His dad hesitated before answering. "Maybe. Be pretty hard."

"How rare are Black Hodags?"

"Very. There are maybe nine or ten still alive in the whole world. Of course, nearly all of them are in Wisconsin. No idea why, but they seem to like it there."

"So," Josh said, "if we kill this one, we destroy, what, ten percent of all that are left?"

"Roughly, yeah."

Josh sighed. "Right. We catch it then."

His dad smiled. "That's my boy."

For a while, there was only the vacuum-cleaner roar of the tires on the road.

Josh glanced in the back seat. It was empty. "Dad?"

"Hm?"

"*How* are we going to catch it?"

His father chuckled. "Well, that's the trick, isn't it? I have a rough plan, based on what I know about the Black Hodag. You wanna hear it?"

"Yeah."

"I'm going to try to knock it out; then, hogtie it, and throw it in the trunk. I've got several feet of stout rope back there now. You'd be surprised how often it comes in handy."

Josh nodded.

They turned off the main road, onto a gravel-strewn dirtside street. His dad weaved around the potholes with fluid skill.

"How exactly," Josh asked, "do you plan to knock it out?"

The man held up his right hand and curled it into a fist. His knuckles popped like firecrackers. "With this."

Josh grinned at him. "You're the coolest dad, like, *ever.*"

"I really am, aren't I?"

Josh laughed.

They had left the highway for a country lane. It had been paved for a while, but had been dirt for the last couple of miles. It didn't look much like a road anymore. Now, they were dodging small trees, shrubs, and a profoundly startled raccoon.

"Almost there. You ready for this?"

"I guess. What do you need me to do, precisely?"

"You remember the spear/staff technique I taught you?"

"Yeah. I haven't had a lot of time to practice, but I remember the basics."

"That'll have to do. When we stop, I'm going to pop the trunk. Along with the rope, there is a three-foot Jo stick. You grab it and use it to keep the Hodag from eating you."

"*Eating me?*"

"I'm kidding, Josh. They hardly ever eat humans. Most things won't; we taste pretty nasty. It will try to kill you, though," he said. "Don't let it."

"Right. Easy-peasy. Dad?"

"Yeah?"

"I'm terrified."

"Good. Fear creates adrenaline. You'll need it for the fight."

His dad slammed his foot on the brake, yanking the wheel to the left. The seatbelts snapped taut, keeping them from bashing the dash.

The car spun sideways, broadsiding something solid. It turned out to be a large, low, boar-like animal. The impact knocked it back a few feet.

He and his dad got out at the same time. His dad hit the trunk release button, which *thunk*ed behind them.

Josh dashed behind the car and threw open the lid.

The Black Hodag was on its feet.

We hit it with a car, and it's fine, Josh thought. *We are so dead.*

He grabbed the Jo stick, and spun to face the creature. It was much closer than he expected.

Fast!

He jabbed it in the snout, ramming the soft flesh that was surrounded by long, sharp-looking horns.

The monster grunted in what sounded more like surprise than pain.

Josh's dad appeared beside it.

He pummeled it with his fists, so fast they blurred. It sounded like a rock 'n' roll drum solo.

The Hodag roared, twisting its body, turning toward the new threat.

While it was distracted, Josh poked it hard in the belly.

It whirled and caught Josh in the meat of the calf with a tusk. The pain was instant and excruciating. It was all he could do to stay upright.

His dad whistled, and the beast spun to attack him. He stepped out of range. As the beast flew past, he kicked it in the throat.

The battle went on like this: Josh and his father harassing the Hodag, keeping it on constant defense. Josh bled into his shoe and it felt like fire.

It managed to catch each of them with a horn or tusk a few times, but never again deep enough to be serious.

The beast started slowing down, its breath coming in great, heaving gasps. Blood poured from its snout, which was Josh's favorite target. It favored one hoof.

"Keep the stick up, Josh."

Josh blinked. He hadn't realized he was letting down his guard. Now, he was feeling the lack of sleep, the blood loss, but he forced himself to stay sharp.

He nailed the Hodag's snout again.

It whimpered.

His dad jumped on the beast's back, straddling it, squeezing hard with his knees.

It tried to buck him off, but it was clearly exhausted.

The man rained blows to the base of its skull, hitting the same spot over and over.

Josh fell back, landing on his butt, and watched, studying his technique. He kept the short staff ready, in case the Hodag got loose.

It fell forward, front legs collapsing, its breath whooshing out.

His dad rode it down, still punching.

The back legs folded next, and that half went down.

His dad whipped out his legs just before they would've been crushed under its great weight.

Its eyes fluttered.

Bam. His dad punched it.

Bam.

One more.

Bam.

It was out.

JOSH DREAMED he was at school. He rushed along the halls, growing more uncomfortable. But there were only girls' bathrooms on all three floors. At last, next to the front door, he found the boys' room. It hadn't been there before.

He bolted to the urinal, reaching for his zipper.

He stopped. Something was wrong. He couldn't pee *here*.

Someone knocked on the bathroom door. It opened, and Josh's father stepped inside.

"We're almost there, bud."

Josh wriggled, holding his bladder.

"Almost where?"

"Wisconsin: birthplace of the Hodag."

Josh woke up in the car. Thumping sounds came from the trunk, knocking the last of the dream out of his head. Once fully awake, the pain in his leg came back. His dad had wrapped it in bandages, but it needed stitches.

"Oh good. I really have to pee."

His dad laughed.

"Me, too."

They hauled the beast out of the trunk. It was stuck. They'd had a tough time getting it in there and getting it out was turning out to be worse. Once it was out, they handed it over to a Wisconsin State D.M.R. Agent. Josh hadn't known there *was* a

Department of Monster Resources. He thought the agent had an interesting face, despite, or maybe because of, the deep scar that ran from her eyebrow to jaw line.

"Nice knot-work there, James," she said. "Can I ship the ropes to you? I'd rather keep her tied since she's awake."

"Keep 'em. I buy rope in bulk."

"Thanks. You guys need a place to catch some sleep? There are cots in the room behind the office."

Josh and his dad nodded at the same time.

"Yeah, but first, if you have a medical kit, my son needs sutures in his leg."

"Of course."

"Much obliged."

After a quick call home to let his mom know they'd be a while longer, his dad gave him a local anesthetic and patched him up.

Josh slept in his underwear and shirt. Despite it being a cot, it was pretty comfortable.

He was lulled to sleep by the gentle chirping of cicadas through the windows.

HIS MOM HUGGED HIM FIRST, then his dad.

"You stink, mister. Go shower. I'll make grilled cheese sandwiches and tomato soup. Josh, you can shower after lunch. You don't smell as bad as your father, but I bet you're plenty filthy."

"Missed you, too, Mom."

She grinned at him. "How was your first hunt, kid?"

He sat at the table with a glass of cranberry juice mixed with lemonade. Somehow, these two flavors worked.

"It was scary. Fun, too, kind of, except for getting stabbed in the leg. Mostly, I guess it was tiring."

She hunkered down to look at the stitches in his calf. After a moment, she said it should heal just fine.

"Sounds like a hunt, all right," she said. "Here: use a coaster."

"Wait a minute. You've *been* on a monster hunt?"

She snorted. "Of course, I have. I've been married to your father for twelve years. Dated for two before that. I've saved his butt more than once, I'll tell you."

"Whoa, Mom. I didn't know you were cool."

"Ha!"

He flushed. "I mean, I always *thought* you were cool, but now I have actual proof."

She put the buttered bread into the hot frying pan; it sizzled. "Nice recovery."

"Thanks."

Somehow, lunch was ready at the same moment his dad, hair damp and sticking up, smelling like mint and lemon soap, came into the kitchen. It was the best grilled cheese sandwich and tomato soup Josh had ever tasted.

During a lull in the enthusiastic slurping and chomping, his dad caught his eye.

Josh's glance flicked to the butterfly closure on his dad's cheekbone, then held his gaze.

"You did well out there, bud. I'm proud of you."

Josh felt eight feet tall. He grinned, and brought his dishes to the sink, where his mom was beaming at him.

"Did you hear that, Mom?"

"Yup." She tousled his hair, looked at her fingers and made a face. "I'm proud of you, too. Go take a shower. You've got blood in your shoe, and you're kind of gross."

"You say the sweetest things."

She smiled at him. "You sound just like your dad."

13
———

Josh couldn't focus in class. He kept replaying the fight with the Hodag in his mind, vivid— like watching a movie. His hands were still sore from the impact vibrations down the Jo stick. His leg even more so. He realized, for the first time, calluses were forming on his palms just under his fingers.

I'm getting tough, he thought. *Good thing, too.*

His head snapped up. His cheeks were hot.

"Yes, Mr. Bagley? I'm sorry. I was lost in thought there."

His teacher favored him with a kind smile. "Happens to the best of us, Josh. I had asked you if you knew the answer to a math problem: what is eight times nine?"

Josh turned the problem over in his mind. He remembered that anything multiplied by nine had an answer that always added up to nine. Nine times two equals eighteen; one plus eight equals nine. He also had nine times nine memorized: eighty-one. So, it had to be nine less than that, and the answer had to add up to nine. All of this, Josh processed in about two seconds.

"Seventy-two, sir?"

"Very good, Josh." He turned to another student. "Violet: ten times twelve, please?"

Josh leaned back at his desk. He kept half an ear on Mr. Bagley's voice. The rest of his attention was devoted to trying to figure out what to do about Leandra, and about his dad.

Time was running out.

During recess, Josh got ahold of a soccer ball. He practiced bouncing it using feet, knees, and, once, his forehead, to keep the ball in the air.

He fumbled it several times and had to chase it down, but by the end of the hour, he'd gotten good enough to draw a small crowd. Some of them clapped.

"Dude," said a kid he didn't know by name, "where'd you learn to *do* that?"

Josh shrugged. "YouTube videos."

"Nice!"

On the way back, Josh noticed someone sitting on the swing set.

Leandra.

She wore a short black, fancy dress. Her long, bare legs were crossed at the ankles. She caught his eye and looked meaningfully at the watch on her wrist.

Josh nodded. He got it.

He blinked, and she was gone.

HALFWAY THROUGH LACING up his cleats, a shadow fell over Josh's knees. He looked up. Caleb stood there, fidgeting with his backpack straps.

"Hey."

Josh nodded. "Hey." He finished tying the shoe.

"Heard you made the soccer team."

"Yeah."

"Cool. I'm glad."

"Thanks."

Caleb scraped the bottom of one sneaker along the bench, a foot or so from where Josh sat. "Haven't seen you for a while."

Josh sighed. "Yeah. I know."

Caleb's eyes were wet.

"Do you even *miss* me? I was your best friend, Josh."

Josh swallowed hard. "Of course, I miss you. I just…I don't have *time*, Caleb."

"You have time for soccer."

Josh set his jaw. "Yeah. And nothing else."

Caleb looked at his feet. Neither spoke for almost a minute.

The coach blew the whistle.

"They're starting. I have to go."

Caleb nodded. "I know."

"You'll be okay. You'll make new friends."

"Sure."

"Listen, man. When this is all over, we'll be best friends again. I promise."

He clapped Caleb on the shoulder and jogged off toward the soccer field.

14

SIMON WOODS PUT OUT A HAND, his long arm functioning as a gate. "Hold up."

Josh stopped with a sigh. "What?"

Simon let his arm drop. "Just wanna talk to you. I started training on my own. Kind of. I know somebody: a martial arts teacher."

"Simon, it takes *years* to get good at martial arts. Bruce Lee started when was, like, five or something."

"Eight. I looked it up. I'm ten. That's not much past when he started. Besides, I've got an angle."

Josh adjusted his backpack. The books were askew inside, making it uncomfortable. "All right. I'm curious. "

"You ever play Bad Dudes?"

"The video game? Yeah. A couple times. Why?"

Simon grinned. He was a cat full of canary. "In the game, you start out with basic skills, right? Then, as you play, you learn stuff."

"Sure. Like most games."

"Right. But, there's an option with Bad Dudes. You can focus your learning on a single weapon, and you get super-good with it super-fast."

Josh's eyebrows climbed up. His lip twitched into a lopsided smile. "You're *specializing*."

Simon nodded. He was clearly excited.

"In what?"

"Nunchucks."

Josh grimaced.

"What?"

"Nunchaku. It's a Japanese word. 'Chucks' is okay, I guess, if you have to use it. But, please don't use 'nunchucks.'"

"Why not?" He sneered at Josh.

"Because, it's wrong. And, if you do, I will kick you again."

Simon swallowed. "Nunchaku. I'll remember that."

"Simon, don't get yourself killed doing the hero thing, okay?"

Simon smiled. "Aw...You care."

"Shut up."

"Oh, hey. When's your first game?"

"Two weeks."

"You ready?"

Josh shrugged.

"Yeah. I think so. Between you and me? The hardest part is going to be holding back, not using my strength and speed. Not giving away what I can do. You know?"

"Monster Hunter problems, amirite?"

Josh laughed. "I guess things could be a lot worse, huh?"

"Yeah, but they'll probably get there. I mean, aren't you kind of a magnet for bad guys? Isn't evil drawn to you or something?"

Josh's mind flashed back to Bloody Mary and her lamprey mouth.

"Yeah. Something like that. I guess maybe 'Monster Hunter Problems' is a thing after all."

15

Josh watched his father piston the barbell up and down with minimal effort. Josh tried to figure out the weight, but he wasn't sure how much the middle plates were. And, since it was always in motion, he gave up.

Instead, he was counting reps. So far, his dad had done forty-seven.

"My friend Simon says we're heroes."

The barbell hesitated, then resumed. When his dad answered, there was only mild effort in his voice.

"Your friend Simon knows?" Josh nodded. "That's too bad. Now, you have to kill him."

Josh's mouth fell open. "What?"

His dad set the bar back in place. The count was fifty-eight. He sat up on the bench.

"Kidding. But, please, let's try to refrain from letting the whole world know about what we do, okay?"

"Okay, Dad. Oh, hey, how much weight is on the bar? I was trying to figure it out."

His dad glanced back and shrugged. "All of it." He gave Josh a hard look. "Who else knows, Josh?"

"Just Simon. Oh, and Caleb, but you already know he

knows."

His dad nodded. "Okay. Good. You think Simon will keep quiet about it? Secrets are hard to keep. They *want* to be out in the world. They want to be shared."

"Yeah. I think he's okay. He started training and everything."

"All right. Okay. I'll trust your judgment. Just, please, no one else. Okay, bud?"

Josh nodded enthusiastically. His dad hugged him around the head.

"Thanks, kid. Let's go raid the kitchen; I'm starving."

The ground beef on the counter was about ninety percent thawed. His dad made them a couple of burgers with chopped garlic and onion, and topped with leaf lettuce, ketchup, and mustard.

Josh moaned around the first bite. "Mm. This is the best burger ever."

His dad replied, his own cheek stuffed with food.

"Don't talk with your mouth full." He rolled his eyes, chewed, and swallowed. "And I'm gonna work on not being a hypocrite. Sound good?"

Josh nodded, smiling. He swallowed his own bite. "Yep. Good plan, Dad."

His mom came in the front door. She tossed her keys in the basket and hung up her jacket. She put one foot in the kitchen and stopped, glaring at them.

"You ate it all? I was going to make meatloaf tonight."

They both stopped mid-bite.

"Well," she said, "I guess we can order out. How about the Laughing Dragon? We haven't had Chinese in a while."

They shared a quick look. Both nodded and resumed chewing.

"Good. It's settled then. Oh, and gentlemen?" They looked up. "Next time? Ask."

"Yes, ma'am."

"Sorry."

16

Josh scored two of the five goals and assisted with a third. They won that first game of the season by one point.

After, the coach took the whole team out for ice cream.

"Don't get used to this," he said. "Not every win is gonna come with ice cream. Maybe if we make it to finals, I'll do it again. Maybe."

On his bike the whole way home, Josh grinned into the wind. As he passed Caleb's house, he waved, though he had no idea if anyone saw him.

When he pulled up, the front door was somewhat ajar.

As he eased it open, his senses engaged with laser focus.

He walked on the balls of his feet, quick, silent, ready to fight.

She perched on the edge of the couch, a leopard lounging across a branch.

"Hello, Josh. Nice to see you again."

He glanced around, careful to keep her in the periphery of his vision.

"What did you do to my parents?"

She frowned. "You wound me, Josh."

"Not yet."

At this, she laughed, a genuine, hearty belly-laugh.

"So cocky! Just like your dad. I don't doubt you will try someday. But you may find that I do not wound easily, human child."

He shrugged. "Where are my mom and dad?"

"They went out for a quick drink. Your soccer coach called to say he was taking the whole team out for pizza, and that you would be home around eight. So, since they rarely get time to themselves, and most especially since your father doesn't have much time left, they went out."

"My coach didn't call. We got ice cream, and it was pretty quick."

Leandra sighed.

"Yes, Josh. I know." She began speaking in the coach's voice. "I called. Mimicry is the least of my talents. Now that we have a chance to talk, I would like to know if you have come to a decision."

Josh shook his head. "You said I had time. Until my dad—until I didn't anymore."

"I was being dramatic. Look, Josh, the longer you wait, the more damage the cancer will do to your father. The more he will suffer. But, he's okay right now. Still in peak form. You can keep him there, my boy. *You* can stop his body from disintegrating into a weak, helpless shell of its former self."

Josh clenched his jaw. He felt tears burning behind his eyes, but he held them back.

"You're trying to scare me into choosing now."

"Yes."

He blinked. He wasn't expecting an honest response.

"Well," he said, "it's working. I'm scared. I'm horrified at the thought of watching my dad 'disintegrate.'"

"It's an awful thought, I know."

He nodded. "Yeah. One you *wanted* me to think."

She smiled. "You can't blame a girl for trying."

"I can. And, you're not a girl. You're a monster. A very pretty, very smart, very charming monster. And, do you know what I am, Leandra?"

Folding her hands on one knee, she leaned forward. "What, Josh? What are you?"

He smiled his own predator smile. "A monster hunter. Just like my dad. And I strongly suggest you get out of my house. Right. Now."

She favored him with a bemused expression, an almost-smile. She stood in one fluid motion. Walking past Josh, she stroked his jaw with a slender finger. The nail scraped against his skin. It was painted the color of fresh blood. Her voice was flat, emotionless.

"Stop it, boy. You're frightening me."

He watched her go, his whole body tense, ready to fight. She lingered at the door, turning to face him again.

"Truly, you are your father's son. I'll be seeing you, Josh. Sooner than you might like."

17

JOSH PITCHED his voice so softly it wasn't even a whisper. He knew his dad could hear him. They'd practiced this.

"What *is* it?"

His dad used the same volume to answer.

"A brownie. Subspecies of elves. Technically, they're monsters, but not all monsters are bad guys. Some just want to be left alone; some are even allies."

The Brownie looked a bit like a poodle crossed with a skinny tree trunk.

"And this one?"

"Well, that's what we're here to find out."

Moving incrementally, the man pulled a chunk of milk chocolate from his jacket pocket. He held it at arm's length toward the creature.

It sniffed the air. Its nose bounced up and down, leading its head toward the treat.

Josh's dad was statue-still. The creature reached tentatively with one twig thin hand. The thumb was opposed by five other fingers. It wrapped them around the chocolate, pulling the candy from the man's hand. It took a tiny nibble and tucked the rest inside its shirt.

"Thank you."

"You're welcome, my friend. I would ask a small favor in return if you were so inclined."

The Brownie's face scrunched up, as if the sweet chocolate had gone suddenly sour.

"Oh boy. Here it comes. You mortals never just give. There's always a cost. Just once, I'd like to get a hunk of chocolate, or a can of soda, with no strings attached."

Josh's dad smiled and shrugged. "Sorry."

"Bah. It's how the game is played. I get it. Doesn't mean I have to like it. Go ahead: name your price."

The man glanced at his son. The boy, who knew what was coming and had already steeled himself for it, nodded. His dad looked back at the Brownie.

"I'm dying."

The faerie creature nodded.

"I heard. News like that, involving your kind, travels fast in our world."

"My son," he said, nodding toward the boy, "Josh, will be assuming my place. However, he's not ready."

"I can see that. He is too young."

Josh scowled. "Hey. I'm trying."

The Brownie patted the back of Josh's hand with his tiny, too-many-fingered hand.

"I meant no offense, mortal child. One does not berate the sapling for providing no shade."

"So," continued his dad, "the favor is this: you and your people keep an eye on him. Help keep him from harm. Distract his enemies. Give him a chance to grow into the warrior I know he will be."

The creature tilted its head and shot the man a shrewd look.

"That's an awful lot to ask for a bit of chocolate."

Josh's dad smiled. He nodded.

"It would be, yes, if that was all I was offering. If you do this, ally yourself with my son, you will have *decades* of protection in return. This boy will be a man in the blink of an eye, and he is *my* son. He will have *my* strength, *my* skills, *my* durability. Not to mention his *mom's* side of the family. I have always been cautiously aligned with your people, trading, bargaining. But I am now offering you the chance to become friends, actual *friends* with someone powerful enough to frighten your enemies. They will hesitate to harass you, just *because* you are allied with Josh."

The Brownie chewed on its lower lip as it processed this information. It took another bite of the chocolate. It looked at Josh but spoke to his dad.

"How do I know I can trust him? How do I know he won't betray us someday?"

Josh's dad opened his mouth, but Josh held up a restraining hand.

"Because," he said to the faerie, "I am a Campbell, and we are men of our word."

The small creature spat into its palm; saliva mixed with brownish-gray phlegm. He held it out.

Josh spat in his own palm, and clasped hands with the little guy.

"Allies." The Brownie said.

Josh nodded.

"Allies."

THEIR FEET CRUNCHED through a carpet of brown leaves as they hiked back to the car. For a long time, neither spoke.

"Hey, Josh."

"Yeah."

He hooked his arm around the boy's shoulders.

"You did good back there. I was impressed. Hell, even the elf was impressed."

"Thanks," Josh said. "Dad? I thought elves were supposed to be tall, and beautiful, and, like, amazing archers and stuff."

His dad laughed.

"Well, some *are* tall and pretty. Some are so beautiful it hurts to look at them. Brownies are elves, too, remember? Also, I don't think *anybody* practices much archery these days. Probably more humans than elves know how to use a bow. And, even we don't use them much nowadays, as a species."

"There's so much I don't know."

"Yeah. You'll learn, though. And now you'll have help. The Fae are powerful allies, Josh. You just might survive to adulthood."

"*That's* supposed to be encouraging?"

His dad laughed and pushed the button to unlock the doors on the car. They got in.

"I don't think you realized just how slim your chances were before today. You were almost certainly going to get hurt, and maybe get killed."

Josh paused halfway through buckling his seatbelt. "You're serious."

His dad nodded. "That's why we came out here, bud. I needed to know you had a fighting chance."

He started the engine.

Josh connected his belt to the buckle. "Dad?"

"Uh huh?"

"I love you."

He glanced at his son. He put the car in gear and pulled onto the road.

"I love you, too, Josh. If there's anything after this life, I'm gonna miss you more than anything."

Josh flushed with pleasure and pride. "More than Mom?"

"I probably shouldn't admit that, but yeah. It's close, though. I'd miss your mom an awful lot. But, yeah. I'd miss you more. However, we don't need to tell her that, okay, bud? That's the kind of thing people would rather not know, I think."

"I don't think I wanted to know that."

"Yeah. That was kind of a horrible thing to say. Sorry."

Josh yawned. His jaw creaked and the yawn seemed to go on forever.

"'Sokay. I'm really tired."

"I'm used to driving at night by myself. Get some rest, bud."

Josh closed his eyes and within minutes was dreaming of elves with longbows fighting hideous orcs. They were waging an epic battle over the last piece of chocolate on Earth.

18

_____

FRIDAY NIGHT. Josh shoveled meatloaf, peas, and corn into his mouth, hardly pausing to chew. He was hungry all the time. He knew why, of course: he was growing, putting on weight; his muscles were smaller, tightly corded versions of his dad's. Except his legs—those were a little *more* defined.

He became aware of the quiet at the table, that his was the only fork moving.

He looked at his mom, who was watching his dad, who was not eating at all.

Josh studied him. His dad's cheeks were drawn in, accentuating the bones. Lavender hollows surrounded his eyes. His shirt hung loose on his shoulders.

Josh's fork clattered to his plate, and they turned toward him.

"You need to eat, Dad. You need to keep your strength up."

The man gave him a slow, sad smile. "For what?"

Josh snorted, as if this was the dumbest question ever.

"*Bad guys.* What if tomorrow, or even tonight, we get called up to fight? You gotta eat."

Josh's mother looked away, but not before he saw the tears slip from her eyes.

His dad still wore that sad smile.

"Bud, I think you know this already, but I'll say it 'cause it needs to be said. So there's no confusion, no doubt. My fighting days are over, Josh. I'm sick and *feeling* the sickness now. I've lost a lot of my strength. I'm tired. I'm worn out. All the time."

Josh was crying, too. He wiped his nose with the napkin. "But," he said, "You're a *monster hunter*."

His dad shook his head. "I'm not. Not anymore. That's going to be your job now, Josh; *you* need to be the monster hunter."

All three were crying now. Josh ran around the table and threw his arms around his dad's neck. His mother held them both, almost crushing Josh. He didn't mind.

After a while, Josh's dad eased back. He looked at his wife, his son. He composed himself, swallowed, and nodded.

"I'll try to eat a little. After all, your mom makes the best meatloaf I've ever had. I'm pretty sure I can choke down a few mouthfuls."

His mother dabbed at her face with a napkin. "I'm sure you meant that to be a compliment, so I won't take advantage of your weakened state and beat you senseless for suggesting you'd have to 'choke down' my food."

He wiped his tears away with his fingertips. "I appreciate that, honey."

He ate four bites, declared it the best she'd ever made, and took a long drink of water.

Josh grinned at his dad. "So, if I'm gonna be the new monster hunter, when do I go out to fight bad guys? On my own, I mean."

His mom side-eyed her husband, eyebrows up.

He shrugged. "Well, how about tomorrow?"

Josh's jaw hung open for a second. He snapped it shut before any food could fall out and swallowed the mouthful.

"Really? Tomorrow? For real?"

His dad smiled and nodded. "It was going to be a surprise, but you asked, so…"

"Wow. *Cool*. Thanks, Dad! Wait. What am I fighting? Where is it? Are there more than one? What weapons will I need?"

His dad held up his palms. "Whoa. Easy there, Chief. Slow your roll. Tomorrow. Until then, finish eating, brush your teeth, and go to bed. You can read for half an hour if you want. You'll need a lot of sleep tonight, so no more than that."

Josh, holding back the grin as best he could, wolfed down the rest of the food on his plate.

In bed later with clean teeth and flannel Deadpool pajamas, he tried to read *The Phantom Tollbooth*. It was a favorite, and his third time through the book. Josh's eyes kept sliding off the page. The words danced in front of him, like they were trying to escape from the story. He gave up, put it down, and turned out the light.

He stared at the ceiling in the dark, trying to imagine what tomorrow would be like. He was more excited than scared, though he was definitely both.

Before too long, his eyes closed on their own, his mind drifted away from thoughts of the next day, and he slept.

He got up in the morning and went downstairs. The sun glinted off something by the front door. Sticking out of the umbrella stand was a silver-tipped bamboo spear.

Josh stopped in his tracks. His eyes bulged. "A werewolf?"

"Good guess, but no."

His dad leaned on the kitchen door frame, sipping English Breakfast tea with honey. Josh could smell it. His dad had had to give up coffee, as it gave him terrible heartburn. But, he didn't want to give up the caffeine.

"What then?"

His dad smiled mysteriously. "Right condition. Wrong animal."

Josh thought about it.

"So, it's a lycanthrope. Okay. And it's likely an animal that lives in Michigan, or you would have a travel bag packed and ready to go. *And* if it were one of the smaller ones, we wouldn't be needed. A werefox isn't a threat to anyone, except maybe chicken farmers."

"So far, so good."

"It's not a bear. I'm not big enough to go against one. It would kill me. It's okay. I know what I can't do. So...what is it then? A coyote, maybe? Or a wolverine?"

His dad shifted the cup, so he could clap his fingertips to his palm. He smiled proudly.

"Very good. Werecoyote is right. It's one of the bigger ones, too. Normal coyotes have been breeding with wolves for the past hundred years or so. Seems the lycanthrope equivalent has, too."

Josh hefted the spear. It had a good weight for him and excellent balance. "I'm ready."

His dad laughed. "You're still in your PJs. Have some breakfast. Get dressed. Then, we'll go off to fight the bad guy."

Josh put away three scrambled eggs, four sausages, and two pieces of buttered toast.

His dad stuck to tea.

In the car, Josh's knees bounced up and down. They were both wearing heavier coats., The air hinted at winter.

"A werecoyote! Wow. This is the real deal, huh, Dad?"

THEY PULLED off at the next exit. Morning traffic was thickening behind them. The trees were hard to see through in this part of the state, despite the scarcity of leaves.

His dad looked at him as they turned onto an abandoned logging road.

"You sure you're ready for this?"

Josh considered the question.

"Yeah. I think so. Yeah. I am."

"Good. I'll be close, but I won't intervene. I have faith in you, bud. You got this."

He killed the Subaru's engine and popped the trunk.

Behind the car, Josh's dad nudged him with an elbow. "Important safety tip: don't get bit."

"Duh."

Josh retrieved the spear, swinging it in an easy arc, pivoting his hips, and striking down an imaginary foe.

"Come on, Crouching Dragon. We've got some walking to do first."

They shuffled along a faint trail, up a slight incline.

"Dad?"

"Hm?"

"How do you know where the monsters are? How do you find them?"

"Well, I hear about them from my friends first, usually. Though, sometimes I already know. My friends tell me *what* it is —in this case, a werecoyote—and my gut tells me *where*. It's hard to explain, exactly, but it's like there's a line, or a cord maybe, attached to my bellybutton. On the other end is the bad guy. So, I follow the cord. Leads me right to 'em."

"Will I have that? The friends? The magical umbilical cord?"

"Ha! 'Umbilical cord.' I never thought of it that way. Funny. Well, Josh, you already have friends: the faerie folk. As for the other, I don't know. You'll have *something*. We all do. Might be the same as mine. Might not. But a monster hunter finds monsters. It's who we are and what we do."

"And the *were*? Are we close?"

His dad nodded.

"About fifty yards ahead. She's ready for us, too. Tense, crouching. Probably smelled us coming. We're upwind."

Josh wiped the sweat from his palms on his pants. Readying the spear, he took deep, calming breaths, and forced his heart to stay on a regular beat.

Senses alert, he padded forward on the balls of his feet.

From the left a gray streak shot straight at him from the trees.

For a fraction of a second, Josh was frozen. The Coyote, German Shephard-sized, leapt straight for him.

Josh blinked, and time slowed.

The creature hung suspended in air, spittle dangling from its jaws. It still moved forward, but at a fraction of normal speed.

Josh whipped his spear around, smashing the blunt end into the side of the animal's head.

It lashed out with a claw and gouged Josh's hand. It burned, sharp and white-hot.

The creature fell, whimpering, and time sped back up to normal. The coyote put a paw to its head where Josh had hit it, a very human gesture. It eyed the silver tip now pointed at its heart.

The fur melted into its skin. Its snout retracted with a *pop*, and the coyote's knees reversed direction with a sound like knuckles cracking.

It took a few seconds, but soon a naked human girl stood before him. She was about his own age, maybe a bit younger. She covered herself with her hands and a single tear rolled down her cheek.

"Please" she said, "don't kill me."

Josh lowered the tip of his spear.

Instantly the girl pounced, becoming coyote in mid-leap.

Josh leaned way back. Planted the butt of the spear in the dirt and lifted the silver tip. He held it firm with both hands and all his strength.

The coyote fell on the spear. Its muzzle snapped and snarled inches from his face. Hot carnivore breath blasted him. Drool drizzled on his arms, and he was glad of his coat.

Its back legs bunched up and thrusted forward, raking against his gut, trying to eviscerate him. Feathers exploded from his coat, filling the air around them like snow.

Josh scrambled back, pushing forward on the spear, trying to get away.

The werecoyote's claws ripped into his shirt, drawing blood from his abdomen.

Josh cried out. He kicked the coyote in the hip with everything he had. He heard bones snap.

It whined, then went limp.

After a few seconds, it changed back into a little girl.

The spear protruded from her solar plexus.

She reached out a hand, face contorted in agony.

Tentatively, he leaned closer and she touched his cheek.

"I'm sorry. I didn't mean it. I never do. It's the animal. Sometimes, it wins." They were both crying. But Josh kept a tight grip on the spear. "You're a monster hunter, aren't you?"

He nodded.

"I'm training to be. I guess I am now. How did you know?"

"I can see it…in your eyes."

She slouched and went still.

Josh eased her to the ground. He extricated the spear, pushing it through her back so the barbs wouldn't do even more damage. Unfortunately, this meant it was covered in blood from one end to the other. Pulling a rag from his coat pocket, he cleaned the blood from the weapon. He did this meticulously, staring at the ground.

His dad laid a hand on his shoulder; *it should weigh more than that*, Josh thought. *My father is disappearing.*

"You okay?"

Josh nodded but didn't meet his eyes.

"Is it always this hard?"

His dad opened the first aid kit and started bandaging his son's hand.

"No. It's not. But, sometimes, it's harder than this."

He lifted Josh's shirt to inspect the wound there.

Josh held it up while his father wrapped gauze around his waist a few times and taped it in place.

Josh thanked him and handed him the spear. He squatted

and lifted the dead shapeshifter in his arms. He winced, and blood seeped through the white bandage.

"Is there a shovel in the trunk? I thought I saw one."

"Yeah. You wanna bury her?"

"Yeah."

"I'll help."

"Uh-uh. I need to do it. By myself."

They walked toward the car. Josh carried his burden without complaint. She was heavy, but his heart felt like it weighed twice what she did.

He buried her a few feet down, so animals wouldn't disturb her.

The sun was past its arc by the time he was done, and hints of orange tinted the horizon. He was sweating, dirty, and hungrier than he could ever remember being. The dressings on his wounds already needed changing, which his dad did.

From the glove box, his dad pulled out two granola bars and a water bottle. He gave all of it to Josh, who devoured the food, along with half the water.

He handed the bottle to his dad, who nodded his thanks and drank some, before handing it back.

"How you doing?"

Josh sighed.

"Hurts. But, I'm better. A little bit anyway. I guess I never thought about it, you know? That a monster could also be a kid. It's kind of awful."

"Yeah. It is."

"Can we go home now, Dad? I wanna take a shower, give Mom a hug, and eat ice cream. Can I please have ice cream when we get home?"

"Sure thing, bud. Three scoops. Big ones."

Josh managed a small smile.

"I never get three scoops."

"Special occasion, kiddo. Very, very special occasion. I am *so* proud of you."

Thanks, Dad. You know what?"

"Hm?"

"For the first time, I really feel like I might be able to do this, to fill your shoes."

"I don't know. I have some pretty big shoes, kid."

Josh smiled wider this time.

"Not as big as they were yesterday."

His dad chuckled.

"Sure, they are. You only think they're not because, today, you have bigger feet."

Josh took a long pull from the bottle.

"Yeah. That's probably it." He stared out the window. "I'm gonna see her face in my mind for a long time, I think."

His dad eased the car onto the highway, accelerating to merge with traffic.

"You likely will. Stuff like that, it stays with you. Especially the first time."

For a while, Josh watched the trees zoom by. He studied at his dad in the fading light.

"You remember your first monster?"

"Yes."

It was clear from the tight, curt syllable that his dad didn't want to talk about it. Josh pretended not to notice.

"What was it? Your first, I mean."

The car passed two exits before his dad responded. Josh had just about given up hope that he would. When he spoke, his voice was flat, devoid of emotion.

"Firedrake. Pretty much extinct now. There might be one or two, locked up in an asbestos room someplace, but I doubt it. They're animals, really—not intelligent—but when they reach adulthood, they start fires everywhere they go.

"So, the trick was to hunt them down *before* they became a threat. To eliminate them. The Firedrake's lifecycle, in a nutshell, is get born, breed, and burn. They only have one young at a time, which is probably why our planet is not a bunch of smoking craters.

"My first monster, my first kill, was actually *two* Firedrakes. They were mating, trying to keep their dwindling population alive. Basically, they were a couple of teenagers in the woods.

"I killed them both. I still hate myself a little for that."

This time, they passed three exits in silence. His dad's eyes were glued to the road ahead.

Josh sniffed.

"I'm sorry, Dad."

"Yeah, bud. Me, too."

19

Josh kicked off his cleats. He peeled off his sweaty socks and pushed his toes into the grass.

He closed his eyes, tilting his head back. The sun warmed his face. He spoke without opening his eyes.

"Hello, Simon."

"How'd you know?"

Josh shrugged and looked at him. "Your step. Your breathing. The way you smell. It all adds up to 'Simon'."

"I have a *smell*?"

"Sure. Everyone does. Most people don't notice. I do. I think it's a survival trait. I'm still learning about all this stuff, to tell you the truth."

"I feel ya. I still have bruises from my first few months with the nunchaku."

Josh smiled. "So, you're an expert now, huh?"

Simon snort-laughed. "Hardly. But I've pretty much stopped hitting myself, so there's that."

"What's up? You only ever come out here when you want to talk to me."

Simon nodded. "How's your dad?"

"Dying."

Simon winced. "Sorry. Stupid question. My bad."

"Tell you the truth, I'm pretty numb. I don't know how I'll feel when he finally *is* gone."

"Man, you sound like a grown-up—a sad, messed-up grown-up—who's seen too much."

"Yeah. That's pretty much how I feel, too."

Josh's feet were cold. He brushed off the few blades of grass stuck to them and pulled on his Vibrams.

Simon flared his nostrils and lifted his brows. "Your shoes have toes?"

"Yep," Josh said. "They're super-comfortable, and you can fight like you're barefoot. Kind of like the Japanese *tabi*. You know: the shoes with the separate big toe the ninja used to wear?"

"Yeah. I think I saw that in a movie. Speaking of ninja and other dangerous people, I recently met someone pretty scary. Said she was a friend of yours."

"If it's who I think it is, she's not."

"I figured. I doubt she's anyone's friend."

"If she has friends, I doubt they're anyone I'd want to hang out with."

"Understatement of the *year*, man."

"What did she want?"

Simon shrugged. "The usual bad guy stuff: said I should convince you to quit the monster-hunting thing. Said people were going to get hurt. *Strongly* implied that one of those people would be me."

"And?"

"*And* I told her to go jump into a pit of flaming dog crap."

Josh laughed. He put up a hand, and Simon high-fived it.

"Awesome. Thanks, man."

"I got your back. Thought you should know, though, that she's sniffing around your friends."

Josh tossed his cleats and dirty socks into his bag. He stood and shouldered it. He did this as he did everything, with unconscious grace.

"Thanks. It's good to know. I'll tell Caleb to be careful. I gotta go. Good talking with you. Keep at the nunchaku; before long, you'll only ever hit someone else."

Simon elbowed him genially. "I will. And next time Ms. Fancy-Pants shows up, I'll drop her."

"'Drop her'?"

"Yeah. Knock her out. Put her down. I'm being cool here, Josh. Try to keep up."

They strolled together toward the front of the school. Josh gave him a sideways smile.

"Oh. *Cool?* Is that what that was?"

"Shut up."

20

Josh moved through the barn's obstacle course with ease. He slammed fists, elbows, feet, and knees into the practice dummy. He worked the heavy bag for five minutes straight.

Despite the early winter chill in the unheated building, he was sweating and flushed.

Back home, he took a long hot shower, and poured himself a heaping bowl of shredded wheat sweetened with honey. He was almost finished with it when his mom came downstairs. She was in her robe. Dark circles lined her eyes.

"Where's Dad?"

She answered him through a yawn. "Still sleeping. I didn't want to bother him."

"How's he look?"

"About the same." She paused. "I keep thinking I'll wake up, look over, and see him back to his old self. Your father was— what's the word? *Indestructible*, I guess. He was the strongest, fastest, always the best. I thought he was going to live forever. I mean, not literally, but you know what I mean."

Josh pushed his chair back; he hugged his mother as tightly as he could. She hugged him back.

After a minute, he realized how hard he was squeezing, enough to break ribs. He loosened his grip a little and looked up, not as far as even a few months ago, and into her eyes.

"That doesn't hurt you?" She shook her head. "You're not human, are you, Mom?"

She shook her head. "No."

"What are you then?"

She sighed. "I'm your mother, Josh. Isn't that enough?"

"No."

She ruffled his hair. "For now, it'll have to be. Listen, I'm going to scramble some eggs. You want one?"

"Two, please."

She smiled at him. "Didn't you just finish a big bowl of cereal?"

"I did. That's why I want two. I'm only a little bit hungry still."

"Most parents don't have to worry about their kids eating like this until they're in their teens. Did you get up early to train?"

Josh nodded. "Just before dawn."

She cracked four eggs into a bowl, added salt, pepper, a pinch of oregano, and a dash of garlic powder to it, along with a splash of milk ("for fluffiness"), and whipped the mix with a fork.

"You're going to be one of the good ones, Josh. I mean, really, you already are."

"Have you known a lot of monster hunters?"

His tone was flippant. But, when she met his gaze, her expression was serious.

"Yes."

She divided the eggs in roughly equal portions and piled it on two plates.

They ate quickly and quietly. Josh took all the empty stuff to the sink and rinsed it. He tossed his mom a bemused smirk.

She arched an eyebrow. "What?"

"You make the best scrambled eggs in the world."

"Thank you."

"It's almost…supernatural."

She laughed, rolled her eyes, and shook her head. "Go brush your teeth, goofball."

21

"RAISE your hand if you can hear my voice," Mr. Bagley said in a quiet, yet clear and authoritative tone.

More than half the kids raised their hands. The others were talking, doodling, and putting things in their desks.

"Raise two hands if you are ready to listen."

Everyone with one hand already up raised the other. Several other kids caught on, and within a few more seconds, all the kids in the fourth grade had both hands up.

"Thank you. You may put down your hands now. I know this is highly unusual, but we had a student transfer in mid-year, and I would like you all to make her feel welcome. Try to imagine how difficult it must be, moving to a new town, away from all your friends. Imagine how you would feel, your first day in a new school. Now, with that thought firmly in your mind, please allow me to introduce you to..." The door opened. "Kimera Xinh."

The girl took a tentative step into the room. She wore jeans with thinning knees, and a long-sleeved crew neck with a Yin-Yang symbol taking up most of the front. It was silver on black. Her hair hung in braids strung with gold and silver beads.

Someone stage-whispered, "She's Chinese."

Mr. Bagley cleared his throat.

"She's Vietnamese, actually, Michael. Kimera, you can sit right over here next to the boy who, while mostly very nice, seems to have lost his understanding of tact."

Michael flushed, and stammered an apologetic greeting to the new girl. She nodded and took the desk next to his.

Josh, a few desks away, sneezed.

"*Gesundheit,*" Mr. Bagley said. "Do you feel a cold coming on, Josh? Need to go see the nurse?"

"No, sir. Thank you. Just had a nose-tickle. It's gone now."

The truth was, Kimera didn't smell human. He had no idea what she might be but was just about *positive* it was not a nine-year-old girl.

As if she could read his thoughts, Kimera looked straight at him. Her lip curled up on one side, and she winked.

What was that? Was she his enemy, slyly letting him know that she knew who he was? Or was she an ally trying to reassure him that she had his back? Or something else entirely? Not knowing was infuriating.

He blinked at her, refusing to allow his confusion to show on his face. He would play it cool for now. Josh kept her in the periphery of his awareness while he focused on writing out all fifty state capitals; he had trouble with Iowa and Wisconsin, in particular.

He half-expected her to be waiting for him when school got out, but Caleb was, instead.

"Hey," Josh said. "You okay?"

Caleb nodded. "Yeah. My dad got us a trampoline. It's a used one, so it was pretty cheap, but it's big. Fun, too. I jump on it pretty much every day. It warms me up really fast."

It was late November, and they'd already had a few flurries.

"That's cool."

Caleb shuffled his feet. "You could, um, come over and try it out," he said. "You know, if you want to."

Josh started to say how he didn't have any free time but

stopped himself. He remembered Simon's visit from Leandra. He thought about the new kid, who was an unknown and potentially dangerous element. About how he could lose his father any day now. *Life's too short*, he thought.

"Yeah. Okay. I'll do that."

Caleb goggled at him for a moment. "Really? You will? I thought—"

Josh cut him off. "How about now? I can push training back for an hour."

Caleb beamed. He clapped Josh on the shoulder. "Awesome! Maybe I can convince my mom to make hot apple cider."

"Mm. Come on. Race ya."

"No way. You'll kill me."

But Caleb started running anyway, his backpack bouncing against his lower back.

Josh laughed. He tightened the straps of his own pack and ran to catch up. In seconds, he was pacing Caleb.

The other boy glanced at him. He started running full-out.

Josh matched him stride for stride.

After a block, Caleb stopped. He bent over, hands on his knees, gasping for breath.

"How fast" he managed between breaths, "can you go?"

Josh shrugged. He wasn't winded. "Not sure. Pretty fast though. A couple weeks ago, I ran in the ditch next to Willingham Road. I was able to keep up with a car for ten or fifteen seconds."

"What's the speed limit on Willingham?"

"Forty-five."

Caleb stared at him. They started walking at a more sedate pace.

"You *ran* forty-five miles an hour?"

"I guess. If the guy was doing the speed limit. Yeah, I suppose I did."

They were almost to Caleb's house, but his friend stopped,

and put a hand on Josh's arm. He looked at Josh's face for a long time, studying it, before he spoke.

"Are you even human?"

Josh laughed. "Yeah. I think so. Half, at least."

"Huh. So, like, your mom's human, but your dad's something more."

"No, man. Dad's human. He's *special*, of course, being a monster hunter and all. It's my mom I'm not too sure about."

Caleb shook his head. "Your family is so weird."

"All families are weird."

"Well, yeah, but not like yours."

"Yeah. Good point."

At Caleb's, they went straight for the trampoline. It was at least twenty feet across, surrounded by tall netting. Caleb peeled apart Velcro closures to reveal a slit-like doorway. They climbed through it and started jumping right away.

Soon, both were laughing and making up elaborate games. They were Vikings, Superheroes, and Ninja. Josh waited until Caleb was coming down from a jump. He bounced himself high and did a flip over his friend's head.

Caleb laughed. "Show off."

Josh bounced a little and was still. "I trust you. I wouldn't show off if I didn't. Most people can't know what I can do, or what I am."

"I'm glad we're still friends, even though we never get to hang out anymore."

Josh hugged him carefully. "We'll always be friends. Even if you don't hear from me for years, I'll still be your friend."

Caleb hugged him back. "Same goes for me, always."

Josh broke away and smiled. The sweat was cooling on his skin. He took the other boy by the shoulders and gave him a serious look.

"You said something earlier about hot apple cider."

"I did. Let's go see if my mom will make us some."

They hustled inside. Caleb blew on his fingertips to warm

them up. His mother greeted Josh with, "Well, hello there, stranger," and warmed up cider on the stove.

It was a good hour (a *great* hour) before Josh stood and announced he had to go.

"Crazy busy training schedule, you know?"

Caleb nodded.

His mom poked her head into the room.

"I thought soccer season was over."

Josh gave her a disarming smile. "It is. I've started gymnastics. Never a dull moment in my life, Ms. Fisher."

"I guess not. Well, it's good for kids your age to keep busy; keeps you out of trouble." She paused. "Not that you're a troublemaker, Josh. I didn't mean to imply that."

"It's okay. I didn't think you did." He wiggled into his winter coat. "Thanks for the cider; it was aces. It was good hangin' out, Caleb. Cool trampoline."

22

THERE WAS NOW a machine next to the bed; it displayed his dad's vitals. An I.V. dribbled fluid into a tube. The tube ended in a needle taped to his wrist. Details of the man's skull were visible beneath the skin. It was like a preview for death.

Despite this, life danced in his eyes. His smile was weak, but warm.

"Hey, bud," he said. His voice rasped. "How's training coming? You doing okay on your own?"

Josh nodded.

The machine beeped in time with his dad's pulse. Josh glanced at the blood pressure and oxygen levels.

"Yeah. Training's good. I push myself as hard as you would be pushing me. I'm strong, and fast, and flexible, and I doubt there's a human alive I couldn't beat in hand-to-hand."

"That's my boy. Keep it up. You likely won't be fighting humans."

"I know, Dad. But, it's not bad for a ten-year-old kid, right?"

His dad's face fell. "Ten? Josh. Your birthday."

"Sh. It's okay. You don't sleep enough as it is. We didn't want to bother you."

"Oh, son. I slept through your whole birthday. I'm so sorry."

"Uh-uh. Don't beat yourself up. Mom and I made the call. It's okay. Anyway, it was pretty dull. I had a cupcake. Mom gave me new sparring gloves. I wore out the last pair."

"It's just...I'm not gonna be here when you turn eleven. I wanted to wish you a happy birthday."

"I'm gonna miss you *so much*."

"I know. I know. You're gonna be okay, though. You're strong. You're tough. You're gonna make it. It'll be hard, Josh. I won't kid you about that, but you've got what it takes. I can tell."

"I don't wanna replace you, Dad. I want you to stay, to get better. I don't *want* you to die."

His dad hugged him hard. He kissed the boy's head. "I know, bud. I know. Tell you the truth, I don't really want to die either."

"Well, *duh*."

They both laughed a little at this.

For a long time, they stayed like that, Josh taking comfort from his father's warmth, his presence.

He wiped his nose on his sleeve.

"You should really use a tissue for that."

Josh barked laughter. "Yeah. I know. Mom tells me all the time."

His dad lifted his chin, so he could look him in the eyes. "You should listen to your mother. And, not just about where to wipe your nose. She knows things. Things that could save your life someday."

"Mom's really something special, isn't she?"

"She is."

"The other day, I asked her if she was human."

"You did? What'd she say?"

"She said, 'I'm your mother.'"

His dad laughed, coughed, and nodded. "Yep. Sounds like her all right. That'll have to be enough, Josh. If, and when, she's ready to tell you more, she will, I bet."

Josh reached across his dad and grabbed a tissue from the box. He blew his nose.

"Does that mean you're taking my advice?" his dad asked.

"It means," Josh said, "that I had to blow my nose. But, yeah. I'll probably listen and not bug Mom anymore. Not about that anyway."

"That will have to do, I suppose. I want you to do one more thing regarding your mother: be strong for her. She's strong, too, believe me, but it's going to be hard on her when I go. It's going to hurt her more than she's letting on. Be there for her, okay?"

Josh nodded. He swallowed hard.

His dad went on. "You'll be okay. You'll hold each other up. You'd be surprised how much strength you can find inside yourself when someone needs you to."

Josh clicked his tongue and raised an eyebrow. "If you say so."

"Trust me. Josh…I'm so sorry to dump all this on you. You're so young still; it's not fair to be facing all this garbage at your age."

"Thanks, Dad, but I don't think it would be fair, no matter how old I was."

The man smiled. "Sometimes I forget what a smart kid you are."

"I get it from you, right?"

His dad's smile widened into a grin. "Yup. Half, anyway."

23

Josh's breath plumed ahead of him. He cocked his elbows and high-stepped, making train noises.

"Chugga-chugga-chugga-whoo-hooooo!"

He stopped.

Leandra leaned on a low stone wall, smirking at him. She wore the same short dress, in utter defiance of the subfreezing temperature.

"Having fun," she said, "pretending to be a normal boy? Pretending everything is just peachy? Pretending your father will live?"

"You know? I was. Thanks for ruining it. That's sarcasm, by the way."

"Yes. I caught that. Time is running out, Josh. I can still stop it, though. I can bring him back to health, make him strong again. But I need your answer first."

"You want my answer?"

"I believe I've just made that clear, yes."

"Fine. Here it is: go to Hell."

"Oh, sweetie. That's a terrible threat. Where do you think I'm *from?*

"My dad says Hell isn't real. That it's just another dimension."

"Details. Just so we're absolutely clear here, little boy: you're telling me you're just going to let your father *die?*"

Josh looked at his feet. He wanted to stand tall and tell this monster-who-looked-like-a-woman where she could stick it. But, when she said that, when she laid the responsibility at his feet, he froze.

A small, delicate hand took his own. The fingers entwined, and Kimera gave his hand a gentle squeeze.

"Don't listen to her, Josh. She's poison in your ears. What's happening to your father is far from pleasant, I know. But it is natural, and inevitable."

"It hurts so much."

She nodded.

"I know. I know it does. But you're destined for great things. And she knows this. That's why she's trying to stop you. You could be one of the most powerful and effective monster hunters of all time. *You* could tip the scales, push evil back farther than anyone in history. But, if you give in to this demon, all you will ever be is a sad, weak, frail, mortal human."

"Hey," Leandra said. "Who are you talking to?"

Josh glanced from her to Kimera. "She can't see you?"

"No. Her kind never can. It's one of our defense mechanisms, a survival trait."

"Can I ask: what kind of…whatever are you?"

She smiled and gave his fingers another squeeze. "If you need to know, I'll tell you. Right now, you don't."

"You sound like my mom. She never tells me anything either."

Leandra was scowling at him. "Josh! Who is that? Who's next to you? I demand that you answer me."

Josh glared at her. "You asked me a question. The answer is 'no.'"

Her lip twisted, half sneer, half snarl. "You're letting him die. What kind of son does that?"

That stung, but he didn't let it show on his face. He gave Kimera's hand a tight hug with his own.

"The kind who understands that, sometimes, you have to let things go. The kind, also, who's going to grow up and be a major pain in your neck. The kind who, maybe, someday, will figure out a way to *end* you, Leandra, forever."

For an instant, fear flickered across her face. Then she was smug, aloof.

"Big mistake, kid. Huge."

He blinked, and she was no longer there.

Kimera nudged him. "Come on. I'll walk you home. We can pretend to be trains."

He gaped at her. "You do that, too?"

"Of course. I've been doing it since they were called 'iron horses.'"

"What? That was, like, a thousand years ago."

"A little over two hundred. Trains are relatively new inventions."

Josh scoffed. "Relative to *what*?"

"Flint knives."

They walked for a bit, both making train noises, and pumping their arms. Josh side-eyed her.

"So, I guess you've been around for a while."

"In one form or another, yeah. Pretty much since the beginning."

"Of?"

"Everything."

He goggled at her. "Like, the whole universe?"

"No, silly. But, since there have been thinking, feeling beings, yeah."

"Wow," said Josh. "You don't look a day over ten."

She laughed. "Yeah. That's kind of the point. Be pretty hard to protect you if everybody was all staring at me, googly-eyed and slack-jawed all the time. To tell you the truth, that whole thing gets pretty aggravating."

"Why? What do you really look like?"

"This."

Kimera shifted—it was like in a movie, where one image blurs into another one—for just a second, she was otherworldly, beautiful. Josh couldn't breathe. It was like looking at the physical embodiment of love.

Then she was a nine-year-old Asian girl again.

"I can't...you...wow."

"See? Can't get *anything* done."

"You're a goddess."

She put her hands on her hips and cocked her head to the side. "What? No. Don't be ridiculous. Gods aren't real. Well, I mean, I guess they *might* be, but I've never met one, and I get around, believe me."

Josh thought about this. "Okay," he said. "Then what *are* you?"

"A friend."

"Again, you're as bad as my mom."

"I love your mom. She is *so* cool."

Josh gaped. "You know my mom?"

"Oh yeah. For centu—Um, for a long time."

They approached his front door. Josh looked at her.

"You, uh, want to come in?"

"If you don't mind, yeah. I'd like to say 'hi' to your dad."

"'Hi,' or 'bye'?"

She shrugged. "Both, I guess. He doesn't have long, does he?"

Josh shook his head. He didn't trust his voice to work right. If he opened his mouth, he was sure nothing but sobs would come out.

He opened the door.

When they got to his dad, the man appeared asleep. His

closed eyes sat deep in the hollows of his skeletal face. They opened. His voice, when he spoke, was a hoarse whisper.

"Hey, bud. Who's your friend?"

Kimera spoke to him in a lilting, musical language Josh didn't recognize.

His dad's eyes widened. "I didn't recognize you. Please forgive me."

Kimera smiled. "You are not at your best right now. Please, think nothing of it."

"You are watching over my son."

It was not a question. Yet, she answered.

"Yes. He already has enemies who are beyond his current ability to handle on his own. Also, you made a pact, the two of you, with my people."

Her voice and demeanor was more like a military leader than a little kid. Josh figured she may well have been that— may still be. If she was as old as she claimed, she could have had hundreds, if not thousands, of lifetimes. She could have been anything at all. Trying to conceive of immortality made his head hurt. Her last statement caught up with him.

"Wait. You're with the Fae? You're one of them?"

She smiled enigmatically at him.

"Most of them call me 'Mother,' though that's strictly accurate for only a few." She turned back to his dad, laying a hand on his emaciated forearm. "I have missed your face, James. It has been too long. Even for me, who sees time as a mighty book, wherein a human lifespan is but a page."

His dad smiled. "I've had a pretty exciting page."

She patted him and returned his smile. "That you have," she said. "And, I suspect your son will as well."

She looked at Josh, who shrugged.

"I didn't ask for this."

"But you did," Kimera said. "You had an opportunity to back out, to save your father's life. Yet, you chose the path of the monster hunter. You did ask, Josh. And we are all so very, very proud of you."

His dad nodded. "Yup."

Josh sighed. "Yeah. I know. And I wouldn't take it back. We can't let the bad guys win. I get that. What I meant was that I didn't ask to be *born* into this. I love you, Dad. I love Mom, too, but did you even think about what you were doing when you decided to have a kid?"

From the doorway, his mother cleared her throat.

Everyone looked at her.

"We did, Josh. We thought about it a lot. For a couple years, we went back and forth, unable to decide if we wanted to bring a child into the world. Knowing, as we did, that any child of ours would not—could not—live a normal life. But, you know what? We loved each other *so* much, and we wanted to share that love with a person we created. And, I have no regrets. Not a single one."

"Neither do I," said his dad.

"Hello, Elys," Kimera said.

His mom nodded at her. "Good to see you," she said.

Josh started to swipe a sleeve across his nose, but stopped himself, and snagged a tissue instead. Both parents exchanged a glance and smiled at him. Josh took a deep breath and let it out.

"Okay. So, what's next?"

"What do you mean?" Kimera asked.

"To fight the bad guys. You said I'm not ready. How do I get there? What do I need to do?"

She looked at his mother, then his father; neither seemed to have a ready answer. She returned her attention to the boy.

"Well, Josh, you have to endure the Trial of Pain."

24

Simon whistled a long, low note.

"That sounds pretty serious. Any idea what it is, exactly?"

Josh shook his head. "Dunno. But I bet it hurts. A lot."

Simon snort-laughed. "I bet it does. Better you than me, man," he said. "Okay. You ready for this?"

Josh nodded. Simon pulled the hardwood nunchaku from his belt. He had tucked it in at the small of his back.

Josh bent his knees and rose to the balls of his feet. His hands hung, loose and ready, at his sides.

Simon swung the weapon at his head.

He slapped it away.

Simon kept the momentum going, backspinning the nunchaku under his arm. His other hand caught it and whipped out an uppercut.

Josh was no longer there. He had sidestepped fluidly.

The sticks blurred on their chain, moving faster than Simon's own eyes could follow. He controlled them by feel.

Josh parried, ducked and dodged, and remained untouched.

After a few minutes, Simon caught the weapon under his right arm and stopped. He was red-faced and breathing hard.

"You're amazing, kid. I thought I was getting pretty good, too."

Josh, who wasn't the least bit tired or winded, shook his head. "You *are* good, Simon. Much better than I expected."

Simon grinned. "My teacher calls me a prodigy."

"He's right."

"She."

"Oh. Sorry. I shouldn't have assumed. You are good, Simon. Really. I'm just, well, hard to beat."

"Good. You need to be. How else are you going to survive everything that's coming for you?"

"Well, I don't know about 'everyth—'"

Without warning, Simon snapped the wood out from under his biceps. Like lightning, it arced overhead on trajectory to smash Josh just above the eyebrows.

He caught it with his left hand and smirked at the bigger boy. "I think I'll manage."

"It'll have to do, I suppose. May I have that back now?"

Josh let go. "Yeah."

With a practiced flip, Simon clicked the halves together, and slid the weapon back into his belt. "Good luck with the Trial of Torture."

"Pain, Simon. Trial of Pain."

"My name's better."

His dad sipped broth from a cup, but Josh could tell he was only swallowing every fourth or fifth time he brought it to his lips. He pretended not to notice, since his dad was making an effort to seem like he was eating well.

"How old were you, when you did the Trial of Pain?"

"Twelve. That's the traditional age."

"What's it like? I mean, if you can tell me."

"It's not a lot of fun, kiddo. I can tell you that much."

"Does it leave scars?"

"Probably, yeah."

Josh grinned. "Cool."

His father grinned back. Then, his face crumpled.

"Josh, I love you so much. It kills me that I'll never know you as a man. That I won't be around for your high school graduation, your first job, your first girlfriend. All of it."

"Could be a 'first boyfriend,' you know."

His dad's eyes widened. A smile twitched at the edges of his lips.

"If that's who you are, that's great. I just want you to be happy. If you love someone, and have strong feelings of attraction for them—oh, and this part's important—and if *they* have strong feelings for you, too, it doesn't matter who they are, or what kind of body parts they have."

"Okay. Gotcha. Can we not talk about this stuff? Try to remember I'm only ten."

His dad laughed, which turned into a cough. He sipped a little more soup and handed Josh the cup.

"You're going to be okay." He cleared his throat. "You're tougher at ten, and wiser, too, apparently, than I was at twelve. You got this, bud."

Josh nodded and tried to believe it.

25

Kimera stood in the doorway. She gave him a long, searching look. She held an adult-sized gym bag; it looked huge against her leg.

Josh nodded. He hesitated. He nodded again. "I'm ready. I think. Let's do this."

She took his hand. Hers was warm, almost hot. "This is not going to be pleasant. Also, you may get injured. Seriously injured, I mean. That you will get *hurt* is a given."

"I said I was ready."

Kimera grinned. Her teeth caught the morning sunlight. "I doubt very much that anyone in the history of the Trial of Pain has ever been ready. But, let's get it over with anyway."

She led him to the thicket of trees behind his house and set the bag at her feet. From inside, she drew a small, metal cube. She held it with her fingertips, careful to keep them away from the edges. It looked to be made up of overlapping blades.

"What is that?"

"*These*," she said, "are RazorWings. Catch."

She tossed the cube in the air. It splintered into dozens of tiny, insect-like faeries with sharp, metallic wings. They whizzed around Josh, swooping in from all directions.

He batted at them, and they cut his hands.

He tried to outrun them, to dodge and duck, but they stayed with him, cutting his skin. Each time was like a papercut, quick and painful. He was covered in them in seconds.

He hit one away, and its wing embedded in the bark of a tree. It was stuck.

Josh ignored the swirling mass of metal faerie-bugs, concentrating on one at a time, while the rest kept slicing into him. Using precise palm, elbow strikes, and kicks, he knocked the RazorWings into the trees. Within half a minute, all the creatures were caught in the bark, vibrating.

His down vest leaked white feathers all over. His sweatpants were more slashes than cotton. The sleeves of his Detroit Red Wings jersey were torn up, and his arms and legs bled all over from tiny cuts. His face, scalp, neck, and ears didn't fare much better.

His hands were the worst. There were so many slashes, it looked like he was wearing gloves made of blood.

He grimaced and cocked his head at Kimera. "Is that all you got?"

She spoke a word that Josh forgot as soon as he heard it. The RazorWings burst free of their wooden prisons.

He dropped to a defensive crouch, but they didn't attack. Instead, the cube reformed, and she put it away.

"I'm afraid not, Josh. That was only the beginning."

KIMERA, who only *looked* like a fourth-grader, bent and picked Josh up by the ankles. She swung him against tree trunks like she was trying to chop them down.

After twenty strikes, she threw him straight up, higher than the trees.

He came back down and hit fourteen branches on the way to the ground. He counted.

Several times, Josh tried to fight back. Once, he connected

with a fist, but she wasn't fazed. If anything, it seemed to make her work harder to hurt him.

Other things came out of the gym bag, too. Horrible things. Some were alive, stinging and biting; and some she hit him with. All of it hurt.

It was dusk when Josh staggered back to his feet and spat bloody phlegm into the dirt.

He had five cracked ribs, a broken nose, three sprained fingers, and bruises everywhere there wasn't a cut.

He stared at Kimera, the immortal girl who had been torturing him all day, while he caught his breath. He had to clear his throat three times. When he could speak, he did so through clenched, aching teeth.

"What else you got?"

She shook her head. "Nothing."

"What?"

"That was it, Josh. You did it." She smiled. "You passed. Congratulations."

His knees gave out, and he slumped to the ground. Now that the adrenaline was fading, he was exhausted. His eyelids weighed a ton. "I didn't die."

Kimera shook her head. "You didn't die."

Josh laughed, winced, and held his ribs with one hand. "I was pretty sure I was going to a few times there."

"To tell you the truth, so was I."

"Not comforting."

"I know. Sorry. But you made it. And, you'll heal. Let's get you home and into a hot bath. Eat beef soup. You need the protein, and the broth will be soothing."

"I'm going to have scars, and a lot of them."

"You will. This is a good thing. It will make your enemies hesitant."

"Yeah. Maybe. But it'll also be kind of hard to explain at school."

She put an arm around his waist and pulled his arm over her shoulder. Limping, and leaning on her, he walked home.

When they got to the front of the house, an ambulance was in the driveway; the lights weren't flashing and the engine was off.

JOSH STARED at it for a minute, wondering how they knew he was hurt. Then, wide-eyed with realization, he turned to Kimera.

She shook her head.

He let her go and ran inside, heedless of his injuries and the pain in his legs. He caromed off the door frame and fell, catching himself with his tender hands. He winced and got up.

"Dad?"

His mother sat on the couch. She sprang up and hugged him close. "Sh. Stay here with me." She stroked his hair, and hands came away tacky with drying blood. She touched the wounds on his face, his shoulders, and his arms. She spoke in an awed whisper. "My brave boy. You passed."

She started crying again.

The EMTs wheeled the stretcher out of the room where James Campbell had spent the last few months of his life.

"I missed it." Josh sobbed. "I wanted to be here. I wanted to say 'goodbye.'"

"I know."

"It's not fair, Mom."

"I know, honey."

They held one another and cried for a few seconds.

The EMTs were at the door.

Josh broke away from her. "Wait."

They stopped. Josh unzipped the dark green bag, just enough to see his father's face. Leaning over, he kissed the man's cool cheek. "Bye, Dad. I love you. I'm going to make you proud; I promise."

He zipped the body bag shut and nodded to them.

One, a woman with a thick Indian accent, put a hand on his arm. "You're hurt. What happened?"

He gave her a flat stare. "Nothing."

His mother intervened. "It's not real. It's fake. Josh is getting ready for Halloween."

"In February?"

His mom got in her face. "I just lost my husband," she whispered. "And he lost his father. You might want to let this one go." The EMT mumbled an apology and helped her partner roll the gurney out the front door. The silence, once it shut, was palpable.

"I should have been here. I'm a terrible son."

His mother picked him up, like she had when he was little. She sat on the couch, holding and rocking him. "No, you're not. You're a wonderful, perfect son. This was just lousy timing. Not your fault. Nobody's fault. Josh, you were training. You were doing the thing he wanted most for you. And hey—"

He looked up at her face, blurry through the veil of his tears.

"—today, you became a monster hunter for real. You did it."

"I know. Thanks. I just—I didn't want to be the only one."

She held him close. "I know, kiddo. I know. You don't understand, I don't think, just how dangerous the Trial of Pain is. Kids older than you have *died*, Josh. But, you made it. I didn't have to lose both of you in the same day."

He hugged her back hard, remembering his father's words. They *were* being strong for each other. They clung together for a long time.

Josh broke away, but he still held her hands. He searched her face, and nodded, satisfied with what he found there.

She let go, grabbing a box of tissues, and holding it out for him first. They both blew their noses and laughed hysterically at the funny noise.

"I didn't think I could laugh," Josh said.

"It's pretty much the same thing as crying, only nicer."

"And, not as messy."

She laughed again. Josh smiled. But then his face fell.

"Mom? What are was supposed to do now?"

She stroked his jaw.

"We're going to keep going, Josh. We're going to survive and move forward with our lives. We're going to train, and we're going to fight. We will do our level best to stem the tide of evil. *That's* what we're going to do."

He wiped away a tear and managed a small, sad smile. "We're going to take on the bad guys." She nodded. "And, we're going to win."

She kissed his cheek. "I certainly hope so."

26

THINGS WERE quiet for almost three months. Most of the snow had thawed, though piles of it still lingered on either side of driveways and in the grassy areas of parks.

Josh had gained an inch in height and twelve pounds of muscle. He was half fourth grader, and half hardened warrior. He made up elaborate excuses for his scars when asked: tiger attack, falling into a river full of piranha, that sort of thing. Nobody believed him, of course, but they wouldn't have believed the truth either. The official version, the one he told the school social worker, was that he fell into the big bramble pit off Ninth Street. He said he'd had to force his way through the thorns to get out.

"But, why go in there in the first place?" she wanted to know.

Josh looked at her for a long time before answering.

"I wanted to feel something besides the hole inside me, where my father used to be."

She never brought it up again.

Buds were peeking out on tiny tree twigs. Gloves and hats were put away into plastic winter bins. The sun hung around for a little longer every day. Spring had sprung.

It was when everything went to hell.

Josh was behind the garage, kicking the soccer ball against the wall. He'd kick it hard enough for it to bounce back to him in the air, and he'd kick it again. The ball hadn't touched the ground in almost two minutes. He timed a spinning, back crescent kick to coincide with the ball's return and nailed it hard. The ball flew over the garage roof, bounced in the driveway, and he heard tires screech. It was weird because they didn't get much traffic this far out.

"Uh-oh."

He ran around front, careful to keep his speed that of a normal kid.

A glossy black sedan sat in front of his house; streaks of rubber stretched out ten feet behind its back tires. The windows were tinted too dark to see in, though Josh could make out breathing: calm in front, rapid, panicky in back.

The soccer ball rolled back to the curb and bounced once before lying still.

The rear window facing him slid down with a barely discernible hum.

Josh's gut tightened. Something was wrong.

Halfway down, the window stopped. Caleb put his face in the opening. Blood trickled from his hairline and from one nostril. He looked terrified.

"Josh? I'm sorry. I couldn't—"

The window whirred up and Caleb had to duck back inside.

The car pulled away and sped up.

Josh chased it. He didn't care who saw. They had Caleb.

All bets were off.

IN HIS MIND, Josh was going to catch up to the car, rip the door off its hinges with brute strength, and save his best friend. However, every time he got close, the driver sped up.

They were both doing fifty when they left his quiet, rural neighborhood for the industrial district.

The car shot through an open gate, braked, and squealed around the corner of a beige building with no windows. A sign above the door read *Styx Industries.*

Josh rounded the bend, leaning into the turn and panting. His lungs and legs burned. The car was parked, door open on the driver's side.

Next to it, Caleb stood shivering, despite the warmth of the day. A strange man held a pistol to Caleb's head.

Josh slowed his breathing, and his pulse. He studied the man while he regained calm.

He was between thirty and fifty, with brown hair shot through with gray. His clothes were tailored to fit his lean, muscular build. He wore a lot of cologne, like he had bathed in it.

The man popped up on the balls of his feet then let his heels drop. He did this repeatedly, like a nervous tic.

A fighter, Josh thought. He smirked at the guy.

"I gotta tell ya," he said, "I was sure Leandra was the one in the car."

The man sneered. "She doesn't want to get her hands dirty. Besides, you're a kid. How tough can you be?"

"Why don't you come over here and find out?"

"Oh, I will, Josh. One day. You can count on that. But today I'm just supposed to deliver a message. Since you don't seem to listen too good, this one is more, ah, visual."

He pulled the gun away from Caleb's head and shot the boy in the foot.

Caleb shrieked. He crumpled to the concrete, clutching his ankle inches above the wound.

Josh sped toward his friend, but the gun was in his face. He stopped, still eight feet away.

The man nodded. "Back off. Stop training. Give up monster

hunting. Or, next time, your little friend here will get a lot worse than a limp. You understand me?"

He shoved the back door shut and got behind the wheel.

"Hey," Josh said.

The man looked at him. "What?"

"You human?"

He sneered. "No."

"Then you're dead."

The man laughed but choked on it. Josh had snagged a pebble from the ground with two toes. He had whipped it at the man, and the stone lodged in his throat.

Dropping the gun, the man clawed inside his mouth, trying to get it out.

Josh crossed the distance with blinding speed. He wrenched the handle right off. *So much for yanking off car doors.*

He reached inside the car instead, connecting the man's jaw with an elbow. The stone flew out of his mouth and clicked on the passenger window.

Josh snagged the pistol, turned it toward the man and fired all eleven remaining shots, point-blank into his chest.

Bluish-black blood oozed out.

"Goblin. I should have known."

The goblin reached across the seat with a pained expression. He was still very much alive and trying to reach a sheathed knife.

Josh grabbed his shirt collar and hauled him out of the car.

"Being strong and fast? Important, sure. Being able to take a hit? Vital. But the most important thing? Research. Know your enemy."

Josh yanked up the creature's left arm, exposing his ribs. He hammer-punched him, just below the armpit, five solid blows.

The guy's eyes went wide. His face turned gray.

He died.

Josh popped the trunk. He hefted the dead goblin into it and closed the lid.

Gently, he lifted Caleb and strapped him into the front passenger seat. He got behind the wheel and closed the door.

Caleb looked at him through eyes filled with pain and shock. "Josh? Do you know how to drive?"

Josh shrugged. "How hard can it be?"

It wasn't long before he knew *exactly* how hard driving a car could be. Though the hospital was only three miles away, the car arrived there with nine new dents and a flat tire.

Josh limped it to the curb, careful not to block the ambulance lane. He carried Caleb into the ER.

"My friend's been shot!"

Every head turned toward him. A nurse bustled over. She was deeply tanned and wore her hair in dreadlocks. "Where?"

"My foot," Caleb groaned. The nurse used L-shaped scissors to cut away his shoe. "Aw, man. This is my favorite pair."

"Look on the bright side, kiddo," she said. "You'll have a great story to tell your friends."

"Finally, something exciting happens to me and not Josh." He smiled weakly.

The nurse glanced at Josh, who was still holding his friend as if he weighed no more than a kitten.

"Yeah. I'm Josh."

"You have a lot of scars, Josh."

He shrugged. "I'm accident-prone."

She gave him a look but didn't press the matter.

"We need to get this numbed and stitched up. I'll get a gurney."

She wheeled Caleb to a curtained-off room, packed his wound with gauze, and told them the doctor would be in shortly.

"Josh?"

"Yeah, buddy?"

"How am I supposed to explain this to my parents?"

"You tell them the truth."

"Are you *nuts?*"

"No. Listen. Not the whole truth, obviously. You tell them that a crazy guy tried to get you in his car, which happened, right?" Caleb nodded. "You resisted. He pulled a gun. It went off, and you got shot in the foot. He panicked and drove away."

"That's…actually pretty good."

"Thanks."

The doctor came in, looking at the boys over his glasses. While he inspected Caleb's wound, he asked a lot of questions. Once he had the foot numb, he pulled the edges of the hole together with his fingers and threaded stitches through the skin.

"You're lucky, young man. The bullet missed all the bones in your foot, as it only grazed the edge. This should heal nicely, with very little scarring."

"I think I might throw up."

The doctor handed him a bed pan.

"One other thing, boys: by law, we have to report all gunshot wounds to the police. I had to call them, and you have to stay right here until they come. It's unlikely you're in any kind of trouble, but the hospital has to follow procedure."

Josh nodded and said they understood. He asked to use the phone; the doctor showed him where it was on the wall and explained how to get an outside line.

When he was gone, Josh dialed nine and then his mom's number. He told her the story they planned to tell the police and what room of the hospital they were in.

"Were you wounded, too?"

"No. Only Caleb. But, Mom? You should see the other guy!"

She laughed, said she was on her way and hung up.

"How's your foot?"

Caleb shrugged. "Feels smaller, somehow. Tighter. At least it doesn't hurt anymore."

"Small favors, right?"

"Right."

They were quiet for a while. Josh watched the fluid in the IV bag as it dripped toward his friend's hand. *Getting real tired of seeing people I love hooked up to these.*

"You were never supposed to get involved." His voice cracked with emotion. "I stayed away from you so you wouldn't get hurt."

Caleb put his free hand on Josh's forearm. He ran his thumb over the scar tissue there.

"I know. I've always known you were trying to protect me. But, Josh…you know I'd take a bullet for you."

He smiled at his own joke.

Josh shook his head and returned the smile. "Not funny."

"Yes, it was."

Both laughed.

"Yeah. Okay. It was. Let's hope it's just the one, though. Cool?"

"Yeah. Cool."

Out of nowhere, Caleb punched him.

"What was that for?"

"Because I've missed you, you big jerk.

"Caleb, I—"

He didn't know what to say. Voices in the hall saved him from having to figure it out.

The doctor was back. He stood in the doorway and rapped on the wall with his knuckles. He pushed the curtain wide.

A uniformed, youngish, broad-shouldered police officer stood next to him.

Caleb glanced at his sidearm and shuddered.

The cop noticed and gave him a kind smile, holding up both palms.

"Not to worry, big fella. That's going to stay right where it is. You mind if I sit?"

Caleb shook his head.

Josh moved from the chair to sit next to his friend on the bed.

The cop sat, back straight, in the chair. He asked Caleb if he was okay talking about what happened.

"Yeah. I'm okay." He took a deep breath and told him the story he and Josh had invented.

The officer listened, took notes, and thanked him. Then he looked Josh in the eye.

Josh could see a spark there: a knowing, cunning twinkle.

"The only thing I don't understand," the cop said "is how did the guy's car end up here at the hospital, badly dented, with blood in the passenger seat and some unidentified black fluid in the driver's seat. Fluid that also appears to be on the back of your shirt, Josh."

Josh and Caleb exchanged panicked glances. *Uh-oh.* He'd forgotten about the car.

"Um…"

The cop cleared his throat. "There's also the matter of what I found in the trunk."

"Oh crap," Caleb whispered.

"Uh huh. You maybe wanna rethink your story now, big fella?"

Caleb swallowed hard. He threw a pleading glance at Josh, who dropped his head and sighed. When he looked up, the cop was watching him.

Josh shook his head. "You wouldn't believe me."

"Try me."

"The guy in the trunk is a goblin. They are dark, violent fae — monsters. He was the one who shot Caleb in the foot, and he did it to hurt me. I killed him."

"What?" It was the doctor. Josh had forgotten he was in the room.

"Would you mind," the cop said, "going to check on your other patients for a while?"

He left, and the cop returned his considerable focus to Josh.

"Why did the—*goblin*, was it—want to hurt you?"

"My name is Josh Campbell. I'm a monster hunter, like my

father before me and his father before him. I take down the bad guys, kind of like you."

"Josh," Caleb said, wide-eyed, "you can't just *tell* him."

Josh sook his head and smiled sadly. "How are we supposed to explain the dead goblin, Caleb? Besides, I think he's a good guy. I can kind of sense it these days. Isn't that right, Officer Kirkpatrick?"

The cop raised his eyebrows. Then his eyes flicked to the nametag on his shirt and he smiled at Josh.

"You've got sharp eyes. How do you know I'm a good guy? I may not be, you know."

"I can *smell* evil, sir. Also, if you thought we were trouble, you would've been a lot less nice. You probably figured we were just a couple of kids who got into something over our heads."

"Aren't you?"

"No. Caleb, maybe. But the goblin was no real threat to me. Ten of them, all armed, might have a chance, though they would suffer heavy losses, too."

He was stating facts, but even to him it sounded like bragging.

Kirkpatrick gave him a long, appraising look. "So, what is the real threat?"

Caleb and Josh spoke at once.

"Leandra."

"She's a demon," Josh said. "Or, at least that's a convenient word for what she is. Powerful, cunning, evil, dangerous. Bad news."

Kirkpatrick nodded. "This is a lot to process, guys. If I hadn't seen the guy in the trunk, who is very clearly *not* a human being, I wouldn't believe a word of it. I'm still pretty sure I don't believe in demons."

"No one is asking you to," Josh said. "Just that you don't tell Caleb's parents the truth. It's better if they think he had a narrow escape with a psychopath."

"I'm not normally one to stretch the truth, young man.

However, I don't see how this particular truth would be believed anyway. How many monster hunters are out there? And are they all kids?"

Josh shrugged. "In the whole world? Maybe six, seven hundred. And, no: very few are kids. My dad died young, so my training was rushed. Accelerated. That's a better word."

The cop nodded. "Okay. And, how many monsters?"

"Millions."

The man whistled. "Hardly seems fair."

"It's enough. It has to be."

"Josh? Caleb? Are you okay?"

The boys and the cop turned as one toward the door.

Josh's mom came in. She nodded toward the cop, an adult sort of greeting, and hugged her son. Then she put a hand on Caleb's shoulder.

"You okay?" He nodded. "Thank goodness. How scary, to go through what you did."

"It's okay, Mom. He knows. He found the goblin in the trunk."

She gave Kirkpatrick a long look, seemed satisfied with what she saw, and nodded.

"Did she really think *one* goblin was going to take you out?"

"No, Mom. But he was enough to hurt Caleb. He was supposed to leave me crying over my wounded friend. But I didn't let him get away. I'm sure her next attempt would be more aggressive and dangerous."

She arched a well-sculpted eyebrow. "'Would be?'"

"I'm not going to give Leandra the chance to organize another attack on me or anyone I care about. I'm bringing the fight to her."

She nodded. "Probably a good move. But you'll need back-up."

Kirkpatrick chuckled. He looked at Josh's mother. "This is all real, isn't it? Monsters? Demons? And, you're a part of it?"

"Yes."

"Wow."

Caleb laughed. "I know, right?"

"Well, I guess you can count me in then," Kirkpatrick said.

"I don't think you understand what you're offering."

"Well, Josh, I can keep a level head in dangerous situations and, you may have noticed, I am armed."

"Some things," Josh's mom said, "are bulletproof."

He smiled. "Then point me at the ones that aren't."

Josh put out his hand and the man shook it. His eyes widened at the boy's grip, though Josh was careful not to hurt him.

When the doctor returned, Josh's mom and the cop convinced him that the boys' imagination had gotten out of hand, and he seemed to believe them. Or at least to pretend to believe them.

Caleb rode to the exit in a wheelchair, pushed by Josh. He climbed in the back seat of the police car, and Kirkpatrick handed his mom a business card.

"Call me when you need me."

She smiled at him. "*If we* need you, we will."

"Works for me."

He stepped back, and she pulled away. They were quiet for a time, listening to the wheels hum along the road and soft rock on the radio.

"Mom?"

"Hm?"

"I think he likes you."

"What? Who?"

"The cop. Officer Kirkpatrick. He was looking at you with a sort of *I think she's pretty* kind of look on his face."

She blushed. "Josh!"

"What? He seems like a good guy. I don't mind if you want to go out with him."

She laughed, a short, forced bark, made more of bitterness than humor. "I'm glad you approve, honey, but I'm not at all sure I'm ready to start dating anyone, nice or not."

"Me either," Josh said.

This got them both laughing, and the conversation turned to what they were going to eat once they got home. Josh wondered how Caleb's parents might react to his being shot in the foot.

27

"LET ME GET THIS STRAIGHT," Simon said. "You got some kind of immortal goddess-type who's disguised as a ten-year-old girl, maybe a cop, and, of course, me on your side."

Josh nodded, a slight smile on his lips. "And my mom, who is sort of an unknown, but I think she's tough. Which is just weird, because she's my mom."

Simon took a bite of the protein bar was eating. He spoke around it. "*My* mom's special power is making the most amazing spaghetti sauce. Might not seem like a big deal to you, but I really like spaghetti."

Josh laughed. "Don't underestimate the power of a good spaghetti sauce, man."

"Ha! Right." Simon shook his head, grinning. "You don't have to make me feel better, you know; I'm comfortable being the sidekick to your hero. You know why?"

Josh shook his head. He took a long pull from the bottle of sweet, cold green tea. "Why?"

Simon blew on his nails and buffed them on his shirt. He looked smug. "No powers. I'm a bad dude because I *train* to be one. I work for it."

"Dude, I train, like *every day*."

Simon held up a dismissive palm. "No powers." He pointed to himself. Then, he turned his finger toward Josh. "Powers."

Josh laughed. "Okay. You win. I hereby proclaim you *Sidekick of the Year*."

"'Proclaim?'"

"I was trying to sound all official and stuff."

Simon toasted him with his empty wrapper. "Very impressive, sir."

Josh executed an elaborate bow. "Thank you."

He finished the tea, pocketing the capped bottle. Whatever else his mother might be capable of, she had certainly instilled in her son responsible attitudes toward recycling.

"So," Simon said, rubbing his hands together, "what's next?"

Josh thought about it for almost a full minute. He sighed.

"I don't know, honestly. I'd like to go after Leandra, but I don't know where she is. So far, she's been coming to me. Be nice to turn the tables for once, you know?"

Simon nodded. "Totally. What about what's-her-face? The goddess kid."

"Kimera?"

"Yeah. Her. Maybe she knows how to find your bad guy."

Josh grinned and clapped him on the back. Simon said "Ow."

"My friend, you are a genius."

JOSH PIVOTED THE HOSE, arcing the stream of water so it soaked the leaves of the surrounding trees. Some of them still had marks from RazorWings.

Kimera watched him, looking perplexed.

He smiled. "My dad taught me this. Anytime you get a big blaze going, sparks fly around. This way, we don't set the whole farm on fire."

"Oh. That's smart."

She propped four-by-four lengths of lumber, so they formed

a sort-of pyramid shape. Then, with Blue Tip matches, she lit the balled-up newspaper at the base of the kindling. In ten minutes, the bonfire had climbed to almost six feet.

They watched it for a while.

Josh turned to her. "Okay. Now what?"

Kimera reached deep inside the flames.

Josh stared, eyes wide.

She rooted around in there; she didn't appear to be burning, or in any pain. Her eyes searched the sky, while her fingers scrabbled for…something.

Josh wondered why her dress hadn't caught fire. Maybe, like her body, it was just for show.

She stopped, looked at him, and smiled. "Got her."

She withdrew her hand; with it came hair, then a face. Leandra. She looked angry.

"I was in the *middle* of something," she spat.

"Not sorry," said Josh. "I'm calling you out, demon."

She glanced up and wrinkled her brow. "What's holding me? How are you doing this?"

"Magic. I've learned a lot since we last talked."

"Not enough. Not to defeat me. You're still a child, Josh. You don't stand a chance."

Josh shrugged. "I guess we'll see." He sat up straight. "Leandra, I hereby challenge you to mortal combat. Tomorrow, 3:15 pm, in the same spot where I killed your goblin. If you fail to show up, you forfeit any claim to me or mine, and you will be rendered powerless against us."

Her expression shifted from annoyance to grudging respect. "You've been studying."

"Yeah."

"I'm going to kill you, boy."

"We'll see."

She set her jaw, glaring at him. "I accept your challenge, monster hunter. Yours will be the shortest career in recorded history. Now, let. Me. Go."

Josh nodded. Kimera released her, and she slid back into the flames.

Kimera gave Josh a long look. "You did well."

"Thanks."

"I hope you win tomorrow."

"Yeah. Me, too."

28

Josh ended his call and turned to his mother. "It's all set. Or, as much as it can be, I guess."

She opened her arms, and he stepped into them. They hugged for a long time. She broke away, but maintained contact, holding him at arms' length.

"Josh…"

He shook his head vigorously. "Don't. Okay? We both know what might happen. Can we not talk about it? Please?"

She pushed a lock of his hair behind his ear. "You have so much of your father in you."

"Good," he said. "I'm gonna need it."

She reached into the umbrella stand and grabbed an ancient sword. Its wooden sheath, once carved with ornate symbols, was worn almost smooth from centuries of use. The white grip tape on the hilt stood out in sharp contrast. Josh, though considerably stronger than any human adult, still had the tiny hands of a ten-year-old.

He took it from her, loosing it from the scabbard just enough to see the blade. It gleamed, not so much catching the light as lit from within.

"This has been in your family since the beginning. It was

made for your great, great, great, great, great grandfather Calvin. The metal was mined on another plane of existence, forged in the heat of a volcano. It is Demon-Slayer, Devil's Bane. With it, you have a chance to destroy Leandra, to erase her existence permanently."

Josh snapped the blade home, and met her eyes. He winked, clicked his tongue, and pointed a finger-gun at her. "That's my plan."

"Don't get cocky, Josh. She's far more dangerous than she looks. Do *not* underestimate her."

"I won't." He laid a hand on her wrist. "It's like I said, everything is in place. If things go as planned, the world will be rid of her once and for all."

She covered his hand with her own. "That's a big 'if,' Josh."

THEY GOT IN THE CAR, and drove toward the industrial district. Halfway there, Josh responded to his mom.

"It's the best chance we've got."

She nodded, glanced at him, and smiled.

They picked up Simon at his house. Josh reminded him to stay in the car until he was needed.

Simon nodded, like *yeah, yeah.*

His mom pulled through the open gate of *Styx* and parked a few yards from where Caleb had been shot in the foot.

Josh's eyes darted around, checking on the traps he had laid. They were subtle—if he hadn't known where to look, they would have been invisible. He had no idea if his enemy would be fooled, but he was cautiously optimistic.

"It's time," his mother said.

Josh nodded. He winked at Simon, slid the canvas bag from the back seat, and unzipped it. From inside, he withdrew a jagged metal cube, keeping his fingers from the edges. He set it on the concrete at his feet.

Then he selected a blowgun and three darts, careful not to touch the points.

Kimera stood next to him, as if she had been there the whole time. *Maybe she has*, Josh thought.

He handed her the blowgun, which she loaded with a dart, palming the other two.

"Are you prepared for battle, monster hunter?"

He laughed once through his nose. "I have no idea. But, we're here. Might as well give it a shot."

"You do not inspire confidence."

He shrugged.

She edged away, toward the pre-arranged position.

"Either way," she said, "this day will be spoken of for centuries to come."

He called after her. "Is that supposed to be comforting?"

Kimera just smiled, turning her attention toward the chipped concrete where the goblin's bullet had stuck.

For a while, nothing happened.

Josh glanced at his mom. "The cop didn't come."

"I didn't call him."

He cocked his head to the side. "You didn't want him to get hurt, right?" She nodded, without taking her eyes off the spot where everything was supposed to happen. "You *like* him."

She flicked her eyes at him. "What? No. Shut up."

Josh laughed, but it caught in his throat.

The air shimmered, like in a movie just before a flashback sequence. When it cleared, Leandra stood there, wearing bits of shiny, metal armor that left most of her skin exposed. She looked like she had stepped off the cover of a Conan the Barbarian comic.

Josh's mother scoffed.

Leandra glared at her. Then, she smiled at Josh.

"You brought your mommy," she sneered. "Isn't that sweet? Ow!"

A small cluster of red feathers jutted from her right thigh.

She yanked it out, just as another one appeared near her clavicle.

She blinked, snarled, and pulled that one out, too. She looked at it. "What is this?"

Josh shrugged and smiled, as the last dart hit her in the six-pack abs. "Elephant tranquilizers," he said. "Thought it might slow you down a bit."

She swayed a little, shook her head, and remembered to remove the final dart from her gut. It took her two tries to get her fingers to grasp it.

Josh hooked a toe under the metal cube, flicking it toward Leandra. When it was halfway there, he spoke a word of power in an ancient tongue. This time, he didn't forget it after.

The RazorWings spread out into a cloud, engulfing the demon. She stood there, woozy, in utterly impractical armor. They swarmed over her skin, leaving short, sharp cuts in their wake.

She shrieked in rage or pain, or maybe both.

Then, she stopped flailing at the faeries. She stood tall as they cut her, threw her head back, and clenched her fists.

The RazorWings froze mid-flight. They clattered to the ground and melted like popsicles left outside in August.

She still seemed shaky, but the cuts were already visibly healing. "Is that," she said, out of breath, "the best you've got?"

Josh pushed up his sleeves. His left hand rested on the handguard of the sword at his side.

"Nope. Not by a long shot."

WITHOUT TAKING his eyes off his enemy, Josh nodded to his mother.

With a grim smile, she raised her arms in a *V*. In the air above Leandra, a huge, iron ring appeared. It was twenty feet across. She let her arms fall, and the circle dropped to the ground, embedding itself in the concrete.

"I bind you, demon," Josh said. "In cold iron, I hold you

fast."

Leandra cocked her head at him. "Oh, really?"

She reached out with the fingertips of one hand, touching the air above the iron ring.

Josh heard a tiny *click* as her ruby-painted nails tapped the barrier.

She leaned forward, bringing up the other hand. Maintaining eye contact with Josh, she pushed against the invisible boundary.

"Give it up, Leandra," he said. His voice quavered. "It's not worth it."

She gritted her teeth and kept going.

"Yes."

Her hands inched forward. They glowed an angry oven red. She grimaced and spoke through a clenched jaw.

"It."

Her wrists broke through, then her arms. Her hands smoked, charred black.

Flexing her leg muscles and digging in with the balls of her feet, she worked her head and shoulders across. Tears streamed from her eyes and evaporated from the heat of her skin.

She emerged. The skin of her hands and arms turned to ash and floated away on the breeze.

The eyes in her glowing red face blazed out at Josh. Her lips pulled back in a rictus smile.

"Is."

Within seconds, the rest of her skin turned coal black. Her hair fell in a clump to the ground.

Soon she was only bones. A complete skeleton teetered before them.

It collapsed, clattering to the concrete.

Josh, his mom, and Kimera silently stared at it.

Simon stepped out of the car and came over.

"She killed herself? That's hardcore."

Kimera shook her head. "She's not dead. But she is far

stronger and more willful than I would have expected. It takes a lot to do what she just did. Josh, we don't have much time. Are you ready?"

He nodded and drew the sword. He glanced at Simon. "You're up, buddy."

Simon glanced down at the bones.

The fallen skeleton moved. With a sound like a hundred pairs of dice, the bones smacked together. Within seconds, it was complete and rising to its knees.

Simon stepped in front of skeletal Leandra. Smiling, he slid the nunchaku from his belt.

"Hiya. Remember me?"

The skull snapped up to face him. Its jaw worked as if it was trying to speak.

Simon whipped the weapon around and backhanded Josh in the face.

Josh was completely taken off-guard. He went down, clutching his cheek.

Leandra's body was reforming rapidly. Soon, she was shaking out her hair and smoothing her dress.

"What a pleasant surprise. Thank you, Simon." She turned her gaze to Josh. "You've hurt me twice, boy. It's more than I expected from you. I'm finished being patient. Kiss your mommy goodbye. It's time to die."

Kimera pounced on her, arms and legs growing, stretching, tentacle-like. They enveloped the demon, pinning her arms to her sides.

Josh's mom opened her hand, palm up. She blew thousands of tiny, iron filings into Leandra's face and eyes.

The demon screamed.

Josh stepped up, sword at the ready.

Simon got in his way. "Can't let you do it, man."

Josh gnashed his teeth. "We were friends."

"Yeah, well," Simon said. "I got a better offer. Nothing personal." He lashed out with the nunchaku, but Josh hit him in the temple with the pommel of his weapon, and Simon crumpled, unconscious.

Leandra thrashed against bonds she couldn't see. She opened her mouth, wider than should have been possible. Streams of darkness came from her throat, seeking whatever was holding her, probing against Kimera's limbs.

One of the tendrils whipped out and penetrated Josh. It went through his chest, brushing his heart.

It was an icicle inside him. He couldn't move.

Josh's mom shrieked like a bird of prey. Her shirt split up the back and glowing wings burst forth. The light from her wings dispelled the dark tendrils and Leandra closed her eyes tight.

Kimera fell back, elongated limbs flopping like eels. She hid her face against the concrete.

Josh gasped. He could move again. With a twist of his hips, Josh put every ounce of his strength into his swing.

She was gone. He spun around and the sword flew out of his hands. It stuck in one of the tires, which collapsed with a sad sound.

He ran to retrieve it. As his hand snagged the hilt, darkness filled his vision.

She was all around him, filling his nose and mouth, clogging his throat. He tasted cloves and gagged. His whole world was icy shadow and he was drowning in it.

Josh fought to see or hear something through the dark. His only connection to the real world was the friction tape against his fingers.

The sword.

Josh gripped it hard enough to make his fingers ache. If only he knew where she was.

A painful tug pulled on his chest, focused on his solar plexus. He felt Leandra. She was right behind him.

He put both feet against the wheel and shoved as hard as he could.

He slammed into his enemy's knees, knocking her down.

Tendrils of darkness emanated from her hands and surrounded the area he had just been in.

The sword was still in his hand.

She got to her knees. Her head whipped toward him.

He lunged, bringing the blade around, gritting his teeth with effort.

Her red eyes smoked in the corners. Her hair writhed like snakes. She opened her mouth and hissed at him like a cat.

He cut off Leandra's head.

SIMON WAS BREATHING, but he almost certainly had a concussion. A large, ugly bruise was blossoming on his temple.

"She got to him, didn't she?"

Kimera shook her head. "Maybe, but not in the way you think. Simon was in control of his actions. He chose to do what he did."

"But, why? I thought we were friends."

Kimera shrugged. "When he wakes up, ask him."

Josh looked at the dead, headless demon on the ground. He had thought she would disappear or something, but she hadn't. He cleaned the blade of his sword and sheathed it.

His mom put a hand on his shoulder. Her wings were gone, but her shirt was still ripped. *So, I didn't imagine that.*

"How you doing, kiddo?"

"I'm alive, but I don't think I'll ever get the smell of cloves out of my nose. You?"

"Tired."

"Mom?"

"Yeah?"

"Are you an angel?"

She smiled but didn't answer him. "My good boy." She hugged him. "I am *so* proud of you."

"Thanks. I'm pretty proud of me, too, actually."

She laughed. Then she frowned. "I want to say 'it's over',

Josh. I really do. But, today, you made enemies. Powerful ones. Bad people. Leandra had friends. Some of them will come after you."

Josh took a big breath and let it out in one long sigh. "Yeah. I know. I'll train even harder. I'll work my way through Dad's special library. I'm going to be the best monster hunter I can be."

She kissed his hairline. "Baby, you're going to be the best monster hunter of all time. But there's something important you have to do first."

Josh swallowed, steeling himself for whatever she might say. "What? What do I need to do?"

She dropped the serious expression and grinned at him. "Dinner. You have to help me make dinner, and then we have to eat it."

Josh smiled at her. He turned to Kimera, whose limbs were back to normal. "Hey. We did it."

"We did? *You* did it."

"I almost didn't. I was pretty sure she had me a couple times."

"Yes. She was formidable. So is your mother. I had forgotten that."

"Will I see you around?" he asked.

"Likely. Even if you don't, though, I'll be keeping an eye on you."

"Now that," he said with a smile, "*is* comforting."

She walked away and disappeared mid-step.

Josh turned to his mom, who was by the car.

"Before dinner, do you mind if we drop Simon at the hospital? I can't just leave him here. Even if he did turn on me.

She nodded. "First, though, will you help me change the tire?"

"You bet."

Josh fitted the nunchaku in the glove box and carefully arranged Simon on the back seat. He got the jack and the spare out of the trunk.

29

JOSH KICKED his feet in the warm air. The trampoline springs complained at the movement.

A woodpecker loudly searched for lunch in a nearby tree.

Caleb kicked his feet, too, mirroring him.

"I wish I could have been there."

"No, you don't."

"I can't *believe* Simon betrayed you."

"Yeah, well. Seems he was more interested in power than being a hero. You think you know a guy; you know?"

Caleb nodded. For a moment, neither spoke.

"I thought she was going to kill you."

"She almost did."

The only sound for a time was the rat-a-tat-tat in the woods. Their feet were still.

Caleb nudged him, and he raised his eyebrows. "But you beat her...Boss level."

Josh grinned. They bumped fists.

"Boss level," Josh said.

"So," Caleb said, drawing out the 'o', "what's next, O Mighty Monster Hunter?"

Josh shook his head. "I don't know. Fifth grade, I guess. Oh, and soccer. Soccer is definitely next."

"And hanging out with me?"

"When I can, man, yeah."

"I guess that'll have to do. But what about the bad guys?"

Josh sighed. "I'm going to spend my whole life fighting bad guys, Caleb. I get up at 4:30 every morning to train for it. I'll take 'em on as they come and do my best to be ready for it. But, right now, while it's quiet, I just wanna be a kid who's pretty good at soccer. Cool?"

Caleb reached over and pulled him into a one-armed hug.

"Yeah. Totally cool."

ABOUT THE AUTHOR

Ken MacGregor writes stuff.

He has two adult-oriented story collections and a co-written (with Kerry Lipp) novel, a middle-grade novella (this one), and is a member of the Great Lakes Association of Horror Writers (GLAHW). He has also written TV commercials, sketch comedy, a music video, and a zombie movie. He is the Managing Editor of Anthologies for LVP Publications, and he curated an anthology for Blood Bound Books.

When not writing, Ken drives the bookmobile for the library. He lives with his kids, two cats, and the ashes of his wife.

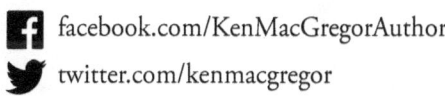

facebook.com/KenMacGregorAuthor

twitter.com/kenmacgregor

ALSO AVAILABLE FROM DRAGON'S ROOST PRESS

Dragon's Roost Press is the fever dream brainchild of dark speculative fiction author Michael Cieslak. Since 2014, their goal has been to find the best speculative fiction authors and share their work with the public. For more information about Dragon's Roost Press and their publications, please visit:

Dragon's Roost Press

The Maiden's Courage
by Mary Lynne Gibbs

The best man on the pirate ship is a girl named Alex.

Alexandra "Alex" Gardner is the reluctant cabin boy on *The Bloody Maiden*, a ruthless pirate ship run by the charmingly evil Captain Montgomery. The crew is convinced she's a boy, and she hopes it stays that way until she has the chance to avenge the deaths of her mother and brother at the hands of the crew. All goes well until the ship takes a handsome captive. Could her feelings for him ruin her charade?

Sebastian Whitley is a young man in love. He sails on his father's ship, trying to find the beautiful girl he's lost. When he's captured by *The Bloody Maiden*, the annoying cabin boy saves his life – and makes it more difficult at the same time. His savior is actually a girl, and if Sebastian doesn't keep quiet, it could mean both their deaths.

Together, they have to thwart a mutiny, get revenge, and get off the ship before Alex's secret is revealed. If not, it's the plank for both of them.

Every man in Elizabeth Morrow's family has either disappeared or died. Her relationship with her mother is strained. Her Granny "knows" things, and isn't afraid to share them (much to Elizabeth's embarrassment). The entire town of Fullerton,

Michigan calls her the "poor Morrow girl," and rarely in a nice way. Her best friends have their own problems: JR's father is a violent drunk, and April has an abusive boyfriend. Elizabeth thinks her problems are petty compared to theirs. Then a dragon named Kieran crashes the Homecoming dance and calls her by name.Elizabeth learns she comes from a line of cursed dragon slayers. It's up to her, as the last Morrow, to defeat Kieran or die trying. Destiny isn't always what it's cracked up to be. The sorcerer who cast the curse is in town, and needs April's life for his longevity spell. She soon gains an unlikely ally in the dragon she was supposed to slay. Together, they must find the sorcerer, save her best friend, and put an end the curse for good.